BASS RIFT

N.R. Willick

ISBN-13: 978-1-959901-48-8

ISBN-10: 1-959901-48-6

Printed in the United States of America

Dedication

This novel is a heartwarming tribute, delicately woven from the threads of love and friendship, dedicated to the two most extraordinary women in my life. To my beloved mother and my dearest friend Jen, who have been the luminous beacons of light guiding me through the intricate maze of life. Your steadfast support and unwavering love have been the wings that lifted me, allowing me to soar towards the lofty realms of my dreams.

Thank you, Jen, for the countless moments brimming with joy and laughter that we've shared. Your friendship is a treasure beyond measure, a shimmering source of endless joy and strength in my life. In you, I have found more than a friend; I have discovered a part of my soul.

To my mother, my eternal rock and the visionary architect of my dreams–your love is the foundation of my strength. The sacrifices you've made, the boundless patience you've shown, and your unwavering belief in me have meticulously sculpted the person I am today. Your presence in my life is an immeasurable blessing, and your love is the unwavering compass that always guides me home.

In the grand symphony of life, you both compose the most melodious and harmonious tunes. Together, you are the cornerstone of my existence, infusing every day with warmth, light, and profound meaning.

The chamber was a suffocating crypt, hidden within the decaying skeleton of a building on the fringes of New York City. A flickering lightbulb illuminated the walls, covered in peeling wallpaper, as shadows danced. The air was heavy, pregnant with the odors of mildew and long-forgotten despair.

In this forsaken nook, amidst the clutter of crumpled papers and bourbon bottles bearing the scars of desperate nights, sat a desk. This wasn't just any desk. It was an altar of insanity, the command center for a mind spiraling into the abyss.

At this desk, The Nomad brooded. His face, a canvas of scars, told tales of a life marred by internal demons. Like the eerie tendrils of a malevolent ghost, his hair obscured his face. His eyes, red and feverish, burned with a frenzied fire. Enveloped in the darkness, he seemed less a man and more a shadow, an embodiment of the darkness that clung to him.

His hands, shaking with an unsettling fervor, gripped a thin, cheap piece of paper. As he began to write, his pen danced a mad waltz across the page, each stroke a reflection of the turmoil that churned within.

"To the Editors of the New York Times,

In the cesspit you dare call society, I, The Nomad, stand repulsed beyond measure. You, who claim to be the sentinels of truth, are but marionettes in a grotesque charade of human degradation.

This city, this breeding ground of deceit, reeks of hypocrisy. Its streets, a playground for the vermin in their tailored suits, hide the rot under their grinning masks. The common man, a mere pawn, is ensnared in their vile web of lies.

Your pretense of civility, your fabricated tales, cannot mask the truth from my eyes. This world is but a stage, and you, its pitiful actors, are lost in your own scripted deceits. You wield your pens like daggers, stabbing the heart of truth.

I see the decay, the moral corruption that festers in this city's veins. My eyes are wide open, and I am the purifier. Brace yourselves. The storm is upon you.

Yours in darkness,

The Nomad"

As the Nomad laid down his pen, a chilling satisfaction washed over him. He was more than a man; he was the harbinger of a perverse justice, a force set to unravel the very fabric of a corrupt society. The room seemed to throb with his lunacy, and the letter before him stood as a dark manifesto to his twisted crusade.

Unbeknownst to the sprawling city beyond, The Nomad's demented odyssey had just begun. New York's streets were on the cusp of being stained with the blood of his deranged visions.

Table of Contents

One

New York City in the late 1970s was a tapestry of contrasts—its vibrant hues clashing with the decay, its chaos harmonizing into a rhythmic pulse. Spanish Harlem was a sensory feast, where the scent of street vendor spices mingled with the tang of city smog, and the touch of a bustling crowd invigorated the soul. Neon signs, flickering like fireflies, punctuated the darkness, while graffiti murals splashed life onto tired walls, their colors vibrant under the streetlights.

Amidst this vivid backdrop, Tony Charisma, born Anthony Marinez, moved with the fluidity of a shadow. Once a bass player for The Funk Express, he now seemed like a ghost of a forgotten melody, his fame a faded echo in the city's endless cacophony. The streets hummed with the music of life, but Tony felt like a discordant note, out of sync with the city's rhythm.

Pausing outside a bar, its neon sign crooning a soft electric lullaby, Tony's reflection in the window mirrored his internal dissonance—gaunt, contemplative. Pushing the door open, he stepped into a microcosm of the city: walls adorned with music memorabilia, the jukebox belting out a disco tune, the taste of whiskey grounding him in the now.

Inside, the clinks of glasses, the murmur of conversations, and the bartender's knowing nods composed an urban symphony, a constant reminder of the city's pulse. Tony's thoughts, however, were a whirlwind centered on Natasha, a vibrant splash of color in his monochrome world, her laughter as bright as the neon outside, her dreams as tantalizing as the city's elusive promises.

At the bar, Mikhail, the philosophical heartbeat of The Funk Express, sat beside Tony, quoting Whitman with theatrical flair, "The future is no less uncertain than the present." Tony's response, a blend of affection and exasperation, reflected their deep bond and contrasting perspectives.

"We're artists, Tony. We live in beats and verses," Mikhail remarked, his eyes reflecting the dim lights, speaking of the city's transformation and their need to find a new rhythm in this evolving landscape.

Their conversation, like a meandering melody, touched upon past gigs and current uncertainties. Yet Tony's mind kept returning to Natasha, her aspirations echoing his own unvoiced desires to transcend the limits of their world.

Stepping back into the night, Tony felt the city's energy—electric, pulsating. Glancing back at the bar, a repository of memories, then forward into the urban expanse, he realized he was an integral note in this vast symphony.

New York City, with its relentless beat, was a complex composition of hopes and fears. As Tony walked, his shadow stretching in the streetlights, he understood his role in this dance of light and shadow. In the heart of the city, every step was a musical note, every breath a rhythm in the grand opus of the streets—a melody that played on, unending, like a timeless song echoing into the night.

Two

The morning sun, sharp and unyielding, sliced through the grimy window of Tony Charisma's apartment, a stark contrast to the dim, forgiving glow of the bar from the night before. The room, a testament to faded glory, lay cramped and forlorn. Peeling wallpaper curled like old scars, and the air was thick with the scent of dust and the ghosts of forgotten dreams.

Tony, known as "Bony" in New York's vibrant music circles for his lean, almost skeletal frame, awoke with a start. His tall figure unfolded from the tangle of threadbare sheets on a worn mattress, each movement accompanied by the dull throb of a headache, a rhythmic reminder of last night's whiskey-laden nostalgia.

Shuffling to the tiny, cluttered kitchenette, each step heavy, he felt the cold, cracked linoleum under his bare feet. The sink overflowed with unwashed dishes, each stained with the residue of solitary meals. The off-key tune of the refrigerator hummed, creating an unharmonious backdrop to his diminished reality. The days of adoring fans and dazzling stage lights seemed like echoes from a different life, a stark contrast to the silence that now enveloped him.

Brewing a pot of strong, bitter coffee, Tony's gaze landed on a gold record hanging lopsidedly on the wall. "*Electric Soul Mania*," a fusion of electronic funk and soulful vocals, once had The Funk Express riding the crest of semi-fame. Its pulsating rhythms and futuristic soundscapes had been the anthem of an era. Now, it hung as a silent testament to a fleeting moment of glory, its luster dulled by the passage of time.

Holding his coffee, Tony eyed the stack of unopened envelopes on the table. Amidst the pile of overdue bills, a stark white eviction notice stood out, its words a harsh intrusion into his reverie. The music that once defined him seemed a distant memory, replaced by the pressing weight of financial burdens and the looming threat of homelessness.

Setting the notice aside, Tony's mind swirled with thoughts and memories. His bass guitar, propped against an old armchair, beckoned. It was more than an instrument; it was an extension of himself, a relic from a time when music coursed through him like a life force. As he picked it up, the familiar contours and strings brought a fleeting sense of comfort.

Strumming a few notes, the raw, impassioned sound filled the quiet apartment. Each note was a haunting echo from a past where music was his universe. With his eyes

15

closed, lost in the melody, the bass was his voice, his identity.

But who was he now? A relic in a city that relentlessly marched forward? The strings vibrated with each pluck, resonating with questions and uncertainties. As the city evolved, his reality shifted and the music that was once his essence faded away. The notes dissipated into the stillness, leaving Tony alone with his contemplation.

The silence in the room felt heavy, charged with unspoken fears and unfulfilled dreams. In the quiet of his apartment, under the shadow of the eviction notice, Tony played on. Each note on the bass was a tentative step into an uncertain future.

Outside, the city was a labyrinth of potential and peril, a symphony waiting to be composed. As he played, the morning sun climbed higher, casting new light on the faded walls. In that moment, bass in hand, Tony realized the music wasn't over; it was merely awaiting its next crescendo, a new song in the ever-changing score of life.

Three

In the labyrinthine underbelly of the city, The Nomad found his sanctuary—a maze of shadows and deserted alleys where he could vanish into oblivion. His mind was a tempest of delusions and dark thoughts, a dissonant symphony that drowned out the world's cacophony.

Enshrouded in a tattered trench coat, he drifted through the streets like a specter. The oily tendrils of his unkempt hair often shrouded his face, a canvas marred by scars both seen and unseen. His eyes, deep and turbulent, were windows into a soul tormented by its own existence.

To The Nomad, reality was a twisted reflection, a world where whispers of secrets and conspiracies echoed in every corner. Every glance was laced with malice, every smile a mask of deceit. Cast out by society for reasons unfathomable to him, he had cast himself as the avenger, the executor of a warped justice.

Each step he took was driven by a delusional purpose. He saw himself as a predator in an urban jungle, its streets his hunting ground. The people he passed were mere shadows, faceless actors in a drama of his own creation. But existing on the fringes was not enough for him.

His hatred for society smoldered like a slow-burning ember, stoked by every perceived slight and rejection. The Nomad's thoughts often spiraled into the darkest recesses, conceiving vengeful fantasies against an indifferent world. Murder, in his distorted logic, was an ultimate act of defiance, a shock to disrupt the mundane rhythm of daily life.

In the seclusion of an abandoned building, his temporary haven, The Nomad plotted his next move. His previous murders had sent ripples, but they were mere preludes to what he envisioned. He needed an act that would resonate across the city, a grand statement to communicate his anguish and rage.

Porcelain over newspaper clippings of his crimes, he saw himself through the media's eyes—a serial killer, a shadowy monster. But they failed to grasp his narrative. To them, he was just a headline, a fleeting sensation. He was determined to change that.

As night cloaked the city, The Nomad ventured out, his mind teeming with sinister plans. The city transformed into a chessboard in his eyes, and he was poised to make a pivotal move. Each passerby, blissfully ignorant, was a potential pawn in his grand scheme.

Yet, random violence was not his aim; he sought a symbol, a purpose. His thoughts circled back to the music scene—the artists and dreamers who thrived in the city's vibrant core. They embodied everything he loathed: celebrated, loved, the antithesis of his own existence.

A plan crystallized, fueled by his desire for revenge and recognition. He would strike at the heart of the music world, at those who soared where he had plummeted. Through their downfall, The Nomad would ascend, transforming from a mere shadow into a terrifying specter.

With a sinister smile playing across his scarred lips, The Nomad dissolved back into the night. The city, pulsating with life and oblivious to the brewing storm, was unaware of the looming symphony of terror. In The Nomad's twisted mind, the countdown had begun—a dark overture to a crescendo of chaos and fear.

Four

The night cloaked The Nomad in its opaque embrace, an ally to his sinister intent. He moved through the city's arteries, a malignant shadow, unseen yet ever-present. The first three murders were not mere acts of violence; they were the opening movements of a dark symphony composed in the depths of his turbulent mind.

The Alleyway Echo

In a forsaken alleyway, under a flickering streetlight that cast an uncanny glow on damp cobblestones, The Nomad claimed his first victim. The unsuspecting business executive, veering off his usual path, was unaware of the lurking danger. The Nomad, his breath a frosty hiss in the chill air, waited with a heart pounding in feverish anticipation.

The attack was brutal, a release of pent-up fury. Before striking, the jagged glass in The Nomad's hand caught a brief glimmer of light. The victim's muffled cries echoed off the walls, dwindling into a ghastly whisper. Over the fading life, The Nomad stood, his act not merely murder but a release, a twisted rite in his personal confessional.

The Subway's Silent Witness

Beneath the city, in the humming, fluorescent-lit subway, The Nomad orchestrated his second act. A dancer, her movements a wordless poem of dreams, became his target. Her grace, a stark contrast to his resentment.

His approach was ghostly, calculated. The sharpened screwdriver, a deadly conductor, pierced her life's melody, silencing it mid-note. As the train roared in, he vanished into the crowd, leaving behind a stage marred by tragedy, the dancer's lifeblood a shocking red against sterile tiles.

The Park's Moonlit Sonata

In Central Park, under the moon's vigilant gaze, The Nomad enacted his third performance. A young musician, his guitar an extension of his dreams, unknowingly played his last tune. The Nomad, hidden in shadow, waited, driven by a chorus of inner voices.

As the musician ventured down a secluded path, The Nomad's attack was sudden, ruthless. The steel chain, a silent assassin, snuffed out the musician's song. His struggle and final notes mingled with the rustling leaves and distant city hum, a grotesque accompaniment to his demise.

Each murder was a message, a declaration of war against a society that had ostracized him. The Nomad, a phantom weaving a tapestry of terror, was crafting a legend, a nightmare whispered in the city's dark corners.

*****

Shattered dreams and hushed voices marked The Nomad's descent into darkness. His encounter with Tony Charisma and The Funk Express was a pivotal moment, a beacon that drew his chaotic thoughts into a singular, obsessive focus.

On a cold evening, the city's heartbeat pulsating around him, The Nomad found himself outside a club where The Funk Express played. The music, a siren's call, lured him inside. There, the electrifying atmosphere was palpable, the air vibrating with the energy of music and dance. Onstage, Tony Charisma, with his magnetic presence and deft fingers on the bass, captivated The Nomad.

For a brief moment, The Nomad felt a connection, a solace in the music that eased his troubled mind. He saw in Tony a mirror to his own pain and solitude. As he frequented The Funk Express's gigs, his fascination with Tony morphed into an obsession, seeing Tony as a beacon in his dark world.

But when the band disbanded, The Nomad perceived it as a personal betrayal, a light extinguished in his darkness. His fixation on Tony became a harbinger of further chaos. He recognized Tony from another life, one he had

22

abandoned, and now saw destroying Tony as a grand gesture to make the city feel his pain, to acknowledge his existence.

Tony's bass, once a source of solace, became the center of The Nomad's destructive plans. In his madness, he saw it as the ultimate tool to shatter Tony's world.

Descending further into insanity, The Nomad's schemes grew more elaborate and deranged. He transformed from a man wronged into an agent of chaos, intent on plunging the city into fear and despair. His pursuit of Tony marked the loss of his last shred of humanity, leaving him a creature driven by hatred and vengeance.

The city, alive with lights and noise, remained unaware of the impending storm in The Nomad's mind. But soon, they would all feel the impact of his wrath, a symphony of terror orchestrated by a soul plunged into the darkest abyss.

Five

Natasha Lopez's life was a tapestry woven from bright lights and broken dreams. In the confining walls of a Bronx apartment, she had battled the relentless grasp of poverty and familial discord. Her parents, once buoyant with the hope of immigrants, had succumbed to the city's unyielding grind, their aspirations fading like old photographs.

But Natasha was an exception. She refused to allow the city's harsh realities to extinguish her inner light. Music was her sanctuary, a realm where life's burdens dissolved into harmonious melodies. It was her guiding star, illuminating her path through the tumult of her home life.

Discovering The Funk Express was a pivotal moment, transforming her world. In a dimly lit club in Lower Manhattan pulsating with raw energy, she found her escape. But it was Tony, the bass player known as "Bony" Tony, who captured her heart. His poetic movements and rhythmic bass lines spoke to her soul, embodying the freedom and passion she craved.

Their romance was a tempest of emotion, two souls intertwined by their love for music and a shared aspiration to transcend their circumstances. Tony, with his haunted gaze and silent strength, became her haven in life's chaos.

On the ultimate day of her life, Natasha awoke with a sense of longing. The morning sun painted patterns of light and shadow across her modest room. Eager to reunite with Tony, she sought respite from her family's expectations and the lurking dangers of the city.

She spent the day meandering through the city's arteries, immersed in its vibrant pulse. Street vendors hawked their wares, taxis honked incessantly, and the sidewalks thronged with people, each lost in their own story. Natasha felt an affinity with the city—its relentless pace, vitality, and concealed narratives.

As dusk neared, Natasha navigated the labyrinth of alleyways toward Tony's apartment, her heart buoyed by anticipation. These shortcuts, familiar and usually safe, led her unwittingly to a fateful encounter.

Unknown to her, The Nomad, his face a tapestry of scars and madness, lurked in the shadows. To him, Natasha was not just a person, but a symbol of the aspirations and dreams he bitterly resented.

Her final thoughts, filled with Tony and their shared dreams of music, were abruptly silenced. Once a simple pathway, the alley became the setting for her tragic demise.

The Nomad's act of violence shattered the evening's tranquility, turning the city's symphony into a jarring, discordant peak. The Nomad cruelly cut short Natasha's melody, rich with hope and potential, leaving behind a void in the urban concerto, a poignant reminder of the fragility of dreams in the face of darkness.

Six

In the shadowy depths of his psyche, The Nomad had orchestrated a chilling crescendo to his malevolent symphony. His obsession with Tony Charisma, the bassist of The Funk Express, had morphed into a vengeful fixation. Tony, in his eyes, epitomized everything he loathed—success, admiration, and a talent celebrated by the masses. Yearning to shatter Tony's harmonious existence, The Nomad sought a cruel retribution, a reflection of his own disrupted life.

Struck by a malicious epiphany, he fixated on using Tony's bass guitar as an instrument of ruin. It was a twisted poetry, The Nomad thought, a cruel irony that would forever entwine Tony in his chaotic saga. The bass guitar, an extension of Tony's essence, was to be transformed into a tool of vengeance, a symbol of The Nomad's rebellion against a world that had spurned him.

Cloaked in the anonymity of night, The Nomad enacted his grim plan. He infiltrated Tony's modest apartment, a place steeped in the residue of faded dreams and unfulfilled aspirations. The gold record on the wall taunted him, a glaring emblem of the success that eluded him. There, resting against an old armchair, was the bass guitar. His scarred fingers traced its contours, feeling the resonance of a life he sought to annihilate.

The guitar, heavy with the burden of its imminent role, became an extension of The Nomad's twisted intent. Draped over his shoulder, it embodied a perverse sense of power. Once a conduit of harmony, this instrument was ready to orchestrate a melody of agony and finality.

Lurking in the shadows, a maelstrom of anticipation and loathing consumed The Nomad. The city's din enveloped him, yet his focus was singular, sharp as a blade. He observed Natasha long before she noticed his ominous presence. Her light, unburdened steps neared Tony's abode. She represented the joy and love that had always eluded him.

As Natasha entered the alleyway, The Nomad's heart pounded with a frenetic rhythm. This was the climax he had expected. Emerging from the darkness, his figure cast a malevolent pall over the dimly lit alley.

Natasha's eyes, wide with fright, mirrored The Nomad's insanity. The horror in her gaze, recognizing her fate, ignited a twisted exhilaration within him. Lifting the bass guitar, he struck with chilling ferocity. The instrument, once a creator of music, transformed into an instrument of demise.

The act's brutality was a cacophony of pent-up fury and despair. Each strike resonated like a discordant note in his vengeful symphony, echoing his life's accumulated frustrations. Natasha's anguished cries reverberated against the alley walls, an agonizing chorus to his violent composition.

Standing over Natasha's lifeless form, the bass guitar cast aside like a spent weapon, The Nomad experienced a perverse triumph. He had perverted an icon of artistry into a tool of devastation, intertwining Tony's destiny with his deranged narrative.

Melting back into the night's embrace, The Nomad left behind a scene that would soon send shockwaves through the city. He had composed the most harrowing movement of his dark opus, a tragic melody that would resonate through New York's streets. And as he vanished into the darkness, he knew this was merely the opening act of his sinister symphony.

Seven

The evening draped the city in a somber shroud, the city's pulse reverberating through the streets. Tony traversed the familiar route to the local bodega, his thoughts a tumultuous fusion of music and memories. The mundane task of grocery shopping was a fleeting reprieve from the relentless swirl of his reflections.

The bodega stood as a vibrant cornerstone of community life. Its vivid colors and the eclectic array of goods mirrored the neighborhood's dynamic spirit. Tony pushed open the door, greeted by the jingle of the bell and the comforting scent of fresh produce mingled with spices.

"¡Hola, Tony! It's been a while, amigo," Mr. Rodriguez, the owner, called out with a warm smile from behind the counter.

Tony responded with a faint smile. "Just picking up a few things. How's the bodega?"

"Busy as ever," Mr. Rodriguez replied, leaning on the counter. "Reminds me of my father's store. The neighborhood's changed, but some things remain constant."

Tony nodded, his gaze drifting over the shelves. Mr. Rodriguez, noticing his preoccupation, asked, "Everything okay, Tony? You seem distant."

"Just reminiscing about simpler times," Tony sighed, leaning on the counter.

Mr. Rodriguez chuckled. "We all get lost in nostalgia. But remember, the community's still here, still vibrant."

The laughter of children playing outside, a reminder of life's continuity, momentarily captured Tony's attention. He collected his items, the present's vibrant beat intertwining with echoes of his past.

Leaving the bodega, the city's familiar sounds accompanied Tony's solitary walk. The streets buzzed with evening activity; each person was engrossed in their world.

As Tony approached his apartment, a disturbing scene in a nearby alley caught his attention—a figure crumpled on the ground. A sense of foreboding propelled him forward.

The closer he got, the more heart-wrenching the truth became. The lifeless figure was Natasha, her body contorted in a grim tableau. Horror and disbelief gripped Tony as he recognized her.

"Natasha!" he cried out, dropping his groceries in shock. He kneeled beside her, his touch confirming the cold finality of her death. The stark realization that Natasha was gone hit him with crushing force.

Overwhelmed by panic and grief, Tony's mind was a maelstrom of despair. His world, already haunted by past demons, now lies in ruins. The ray of hope, Natasha, was extinguished.

In a daze of agony, Tony's instincts urged him to flee. He ran from the alley, his cries reverberating off the walls. Unbeknownst to him, a homeless man observed his anguished exit and subsequent retreat into his apartment.

Tony's escape blurred into a chaotic rush, the city's lights and shadows merging around him. He reached his apartment, slamming the door behind him. Inside, his world, once resonant with music and love, was now a hollow echo chamber, reverberating with the haunting melody of a life forever changed.

Eight

Detective Patrick O'Brien sat entrenched in his cluttered precinct office, a physical manifestation of the turmoil in his mind. In his mid-40s, with a stocky build and a face weathered by years on the force, his deep-set eyes bore witness to innumerable sleepless nights and unresolved cases. His hair, once a rich chestnut, now bore the silvery streaks of his profession's demands.

The precinct was a whirlwind of activity, a symphony of ringing phones, officers' banter, and the rhythmic clatter of typewriters. Walls adorned with maps and photographs, each a fragment of the enigmatic puzzle he was determined to solve surrounded O'Brien's desk, a small sanctuary amidst the chaos.

The recent string of murders attributed to The Nomad had tested O'Brien's resolve like no other case. The weight of expectation from his superiors and the city's residents was palpable, and the media frenzy only exacerbated the tension. Sensational headlines about the elusive killer filled the newspapers, each report more speculative than the last.

The Nomad's taunting letter to The Times, a chilling message devoid of leads, had further heightened the city's anxiety. O'Brien could feel the collective fear and anticipation, an unspoken demand for resolution to this waking nightmare.

Rubbing his temples to quell his persistent headache, O'Brien's gaze drifted over the evidence scattered across his desk. Crime scene photos, witness statements, and other tangible clues formed a macabre mosaic, a narrative written in blood and darkness.

The abrupt ring of his phone shattered his concentration. "Detective O'Brien," he answered, his voice a mix of weariness and resolve. The call brought news of another murder, potentially linked to The Nomad.

Taking down the details, O'Brien's demeanor remained composed despite the internal turmoil. The latest victim was a woman discovered near an apartment in Spanish Harlem. The crime scene bore The Nomad's hallmark savagery but with a disturbing extra element: the murder weapon was a bass guitar, instead of a usual weapon.

This revelation set O'Brien's mind racing. Using a personal item as the weapon implied a deeper connection, either between the killer and the victim, or possibly involving someone else entirely.

Rising from his desk, O'Brien felt the hum of the precinct recede into the background. He was singularly focused on the task at hand. He needed to visit the crime scene and begin unraveling this newest, most intimate chapter of The Nomad's grim narrative.

Donning his coat, O'Brien braced himself for the grim reality awaiting him. Each step out of the precinct was laden with a heavy sense of duty and an unwavering determination to serve justice. He stepped into the night, the city's cry for resolution echoing in his ears.

As he embarked on his journey to confront the latest crime scene, O'Brien carried not just the physical weight of his detective's badge, but also the metaphorical weight of a city gripped by fear. In a landscape overshadowed by uncertainty, he was a lone beacon of hope, tasked with navigating the murky waters of a case that continued to elude him at every turn.

Nine

Detective Patrick O'Brien arrived at the crime scene, a narrow alleyway transformed into a grim stage of investigation and tragedy. The coroner, methodically examining Natasha's body, estimated the time of death and highlighted the brutality of the attack. The peculiar marks on her body, resembling guitar string imprints, hinted at a violent and hatred-filled intent for the murder.

Crossing under the yellow tape, O'Brien's seasoned gaze quickly absorbed the harrowing details. Natasha lay amid the chaos, her lifeless form a jarring contrast to the alley's dark backdrop. The police flashlights cast stark, unforgiving light on her still face, accentuating the tragedy of her violent end.

Nearby, a bass guitar lay discarded, a poignant symbol amidst the horror. Its strings, once harbingers of melody, were now eerily silent and stained with blood. Signs of struggle marred the polished surface of the instrument, telling a story of brutality and desperation.

Someone had turned this alley, usually just another forgotten passage in the city's vast labyrinth, into a grotesque theater. The usual detritus of urban life now lay interspersed with stark evidence of the crime. The damp walls, stained and seemingly silent, witnessed the atrocity within their confines.

For O'Brien, scenes like this, although all too familiar, each left a distinct mark of horror and sadness. This tableau of violence was a graphic and tragic reminder of humanity's darkest capabilities.

The coroner's team was already at work, their methodical approach a stark contrast to the chaos of the crime. Technicians meticulously searched for prints on the guitar and the surrounding area, while photographers documented every detail of the scene.

O'Brien approached Nathan, the homeless witness, who stood nervously under a dim streetlight, guarded by a young officer. Nathan's weathered appearance spoke volumes of a life spent in the margins of society.

"Evening, Nathan," O'Brien greeted, his tone calm and professional. "I hear you might have seen something tonight. Can you tell me about it?"

Nathan's account, though hesitant, painted a vivid picture: a tall, gaunt man, his dark hair disheveled, fleeing the alley in a state of shock. O'Brien carefully noted every detail, aware that even the smallest observation could prove crucial.

After speaking with Nathan, O'Brien returned to the scene, his mind racing with possibilities. Using a bass guitar as a weapon suggested a personal connection, perhaps to a musician or a dispute within a band. The secluded, quiet nature of the alley showed a deliberate choice for this violent encounter.

The coroner, methodically examining Natasha's body, estimated the time of death and highlighted the brutality of the attack. The peculiar marks on her body, resembling guitar string imprints, hinted at a deliberate and personal nature of the crime.

As O'Brien stepped out of the alley, enveloped once more by the city's ambient noise, he contemplated the intricate web of relationships that could have led to such a personal and violent act in this hidden corner of New York.

With Natasha's body being prepared for transport, O'Brien took one final look at the scene. This once anonymous alley had become the center of a narrative that would resonate throughout the community.

Leaving the alley, Detective O'Brien felt the full weight of the case. The city, a mosaic of stories and secrets, now looked to him for answers. He carried the burden of responsibility and the challenge of unraveling this complex mystery, fully aware of the arduous journey of discovery and truth that lay ahead.

Ten

Tony slumped in the chair, a shadow of his former self engulfed in the gloom of his cluttered apartment. The room, a mausoleum of his shattered dreams, was thick with the scent of stale alcohol and despair. He was a man haunted, lost in the labyrinth of his grief, every tear a reminder of the dreams he had once dared to chase.

The abrupt knock at the door jolted him from his reverie. With a heavy sigh, he lifted himself, his movements sluggish, weighed down by sorrow. A swig from the wine bottle did little to steady his nerves as he stumbled to answer. The door creaked open, revealing Detective Patrick O'Brien, a figure of authority, his eyes sharp and assessing under the brim of his hat.

"Anthony Martinez? Also known as 'Bony' Tony Charisma?" O'Brien's voice cut through the haze, firm and unwavering. "I'm here about a murder last night."

Tony, clouded by grief and substance, barely registered the gravity of the words. "Murder?" His voice was a hoarse whisper, laden with confusion and disbelief.

O'Brien's tone turned grave. "Your girlfriend, Natasha... she's the victim."

40

Upon hearing Detective O'Brien's words, a fresh wave of agony washed over Tony. The reality of Natasha's death, already a crushing burden on his soul, resurfaced with renewed force. She had been his guiding light through life's tumultuous journey, and now the stark finality of her absence tore through him. His heart ached as if gripped by an unseen hand, the profound sense of loss rendering him hollow and desolate.

O'Brien observed Tony's crumbling façade, his detective's instinct oscillating between suspicion and empathy. Was this the raw grief of a man who had lost everything or an elaborate act to veil guilt?

The detective's presence filled the room, his keen eyes missing nothing. "May I come in?" His voice, though soft, carried an authority that was hard to ignore.

Tony led the way, stepping over the detritus of his life in disarray. He offered a seat on a worn couch, the fabric bearing the imprint of countless nights spent in solitude.

O'Brien's interrogation was methodical, his questions sharp and probing. "Where were you last night?" His gaze never wavered, reading every nuance of Tony's response.

With an unsteady voice, Tony recounted his movements - the trip to the bodega, the haunting discovery of Natasha's lifeless body. Each word was a struggle against the tide of memories threatening to overwhelm him.

O'Brien leaned forward, his demeanor shifting. "We found some troubling evidence," he said, each word measured and deliberate. "Your bass was at the scene next to Natasha."

Tony's face blanched, the color draining as if the words had physically struck him. He felt an icy knot form in his stomach, the implications of O'Brien's statement hitting him with the force of a freight train.

Detective O'Brien, unphased by Tony's demeanor, continued, his voice steady. "Witnesses placed you near the scene around the time of Natasha's death. Can you explain that?"

Tony wracked his brain, trying to piece together the fragments of the previous night. The memories were a blur, muddied by the haze of alcohol from the discovery and his tumultuous emotions. "I... I already told you what happened."

O'Brien's eyes narrowed slightly, scrutinizing Tony's every reaction. "That doesn't help your case, Tony. Why would you run instead of trying to help or call someone to help her?"

Tony shifted uncomfortably, the weight of the detective's gaze bearing down on him. "I don't know, I just reacted. I had never seen someone dead before, and Natasha...." His voice cracked; the words laced with regret. "I never wanted us to end like this."

The detective leaned back; his expression was unreadable. He seemed to consider Tony's words, weighing them against the evidence he had. "And where did you go after leaving the scene?"

Tony's protest was spontaneous, his fear palpable. "I came back here! I've been at the bottom of a lot of bottles! You can't do this without a warrant!" His voice was edged with desperation. The accusatory tone of the detective hung in the air between them, a tangible reminder of the gravity of the situation. Tony's mind raced, thoughts tumbling over each other in a frantic search for some sliver of redemption. But deep down, Tony knew that uncertainty shrouded the path ahead, and the detective's unwavering pursuit of the truth was the only thing sure.

The detective's reply was calm yet firm. "Your reluctance only raises more questions." Though cold, his eyes hinted at an underlying understanding of Tony's turmoil.

The room, once a haven for Tony's troubled mind, now transformed into a battleground of wills. Detective O'Brien's unwavering pursuit of the truth clashed with his agitated state. The air was tense, each breath heavy with the weight of unspoken accusations.

O'Brien, his gaze never leaving Tony, spoke with deliberate calmness, "We found something else at the scene, Tony. A torn note." He watched Tony's reaction closely, looking for any flicker of recognition.

Tony's eyes darted nervously, a clear sign of his growing unease. "A note?" he echoed, his voice strained, the words barely audible.

"Yes, a note," O'Brien continued, his tone firm. "Partially torn. It seems to have male handwriting on it. Can you explain that?" The detective showed Tony an evidence bag with a torn-up note inside.

Tony's face paled, his mind racing. The memory of a heated argument, the tearing of paper, and the words he had written in anger came rushing back. "That note... it was nothing," he muttered, trying to dismiss its significance. "Just a stupid argument we had. It means nothing."

O'Brien leaned in, his eyes narrowing. "Arguments can mean a lot, especially in cases like this. What was it about, Tony?"

Tony shifted uncomfortably; his hands clenched tightly in his lap. "I... I don't remember exactly. Just some angry words, that's all."

The detective's demeanor hardened. "I need to hear what it was about, Tony. It could be crucial evidence."

Tony's refusal was a mix of defiance and fear. "No, you can't just invade my privacy like that. You need a warrant."

O'Brien, unphased, stood up, towering over Tony. "This isn't about privacy, Tony. It's about a murder investigation. Refusing to cooperate only makes you look more suspicious."

The standoff between them was palpable, the tension in the room escalating with each passing second. Tony, trapped in the turmoil of his emotions, and O'Brien, the embodiment of the law, searching for a crack in the man's façade before him.

"Tony," O'Brien said, his voice a blend of sternness and persuasion, "I'm trying to piece together what happened to Natasha. That note could shed light on your relationship, on what happened that night."

Tony looked away; his eyes filled with conflict. The note, a fragment of a moment filled with anger and regret, now held the power to change the course of the investigation.

His silence spoke volumes, a testament to the chaos within him.

Detective O'Brien, realizing the delicate balance of the situation, made a mental note to follow up on the message. Acutely aware of the legal boundaries he must navigate, he sensed the futility of pushing further without a warrant. The room, thick with tension, seemed to contract around them, amplifying the gravity of their exchange. With a final, piercing look at Tony, he stepped back, knowing that this confrontation was far from over.

He stood up, his eyes locked on Tony. "Listen, Tony, I understand you're going through a lot right now," he began, his voice a blend of stern professionalism and a hint of empathy. "But hindering a murder investigation will not help you or honor Natasha's memory."

Sitting in his chair, Tony looked up with a mix of defiance and despair in his eyes. "You think I don't know that?" he shot back; his voice ragged. "But I can't help you. I know nothing more."

O'Brien leaned forward, placing his hands on the back of the chair opposite Tony. "I want to believe you, Tony, but the evidence... it's not looking good for you. That note, your guitar at the scene–it's hard to overlook these things."

Tony's hands clenched into fists, physically manifesting his inner turmoil. "But it's not what it seems. You've got to believe me, Detective. I loved her. I wouldn't hurt her."

The detective straightened; his gaze unwavering. "Then help us understand, Tony. Help us piece this together. If you're innocent, the truth is your strongest ally."

Tony shook his head, a gesture of helplessness and frustration. "You don't understand. It's not that simple."

O'Brien sighed, his posture relaxing slightly, signaling a temporary retreat. "I can see you're not ready to talk. But think about what I said. We will find out what happened to Natasha, with or without your help. It's better if you're on the right side of this when we do."

He paused as he moved towards the door, turning back to Tony. "Consider what I've said, Tony. If there's anything you remember, anything at all, you need to let us know. It could make all the difference."

With those last words, O'Brien stepped out of the apartment, leaving Tony alone with his thoughts. The silence that followed was deafening, a stark contrast to the intensity of their conversation. The detective's departure left Tony feeling lost and overwhelmed with fear.

Eleven

The next day dawned with a sky the color of tarnished silver, clouds hanging low over the city as if echoing Tony's turbulent emotions. Sleep had evaded him; his mind was a tangled web of thoughts about Natasha and Detective O'Brien's unsettling visit. His scheduled brunch with Bran, a plan forged in simpler times, now seemed like a beacon in the storm that had overtaken his life.

Tony found himself at their favorite haunt, a cozy diner known for its nostalgic ambiance and the best blueberry pancakes in the city. The place, a sanctuary for local artists, buzzed with the energy of creativity, its walls a mosaic of signed posters from jazz virtuosos and rock legends. Amidst the clinking of dishes and the mellow strains of a saxophone, Tony found a fleeting sense of peace.

Bran entered, a fusion of charisma and serenity. His signature leather jacket, peppered with eclectic band pins, and his hair, loosely tied, framed a face that radiated an almost Zen-like calm. More than just a drummer for The Funk Express, Bran was its pulse, the stabilizing force in their often-tumultuous journey.

"Tony, man, you look like you've been through a storm," Bran commented, concern lacing his voice as he settled into the booth. He ordered his usual black coffee and focused entirely on his friend.

A tired smile flickered on Tony's face. "It's been more than just a rough night, Bran. It's... it's a nightmare." His voice faded, leaving an echo of despair in the air.

Bran's demeanor shifted to one of intense focus. "Spill it, Tony. I'm here."

Exhaling deeply, Tony unraveled the harrowing tale—Natasha's tragic end, the detective's accusatory visit, and the incriminating note born from a moment of anger. Bran absorbed every word, his gaze never straying from Tony's face.

"Natasha's gone, Bran. And they're pointing fingers at me because of a heated moment and a guitar," Tony said, his voice a mix of sorrow and exasperation.

Bran leaned back, his thoughts churning. "You're innocent, Tony. I know you. But you're in the eye of the storm now. Be vigilant."

Tony clasped his coffee mug, seeking solace in its warmth. "I'm lost, Bran. It feels like I'm being swept away by this whole mess."

Bran extended his hand across the table, a silent show of unyielding support. "You're not alone, Tony. We're in this together. You've got me, and you've got the band. We're more than a group; we're a family."

They shifted the conversation to The Funk Express and their shared musical journey. Bran reminisced about their past, the unbreakable bond that had carried them through both triumphs and trials. "Our music was our sanctuary, Tony. It's what's kept us together, and it's what will help you navigate through this storm," he said, his tone tinged with a nostalgic ache.

As they conversed, a flicker of hope ignited in Tony's heart. Bran's steadfast support and their shared devotion to music offered him a much-needed anchor. They parted with Bran's assurance of unwavering assistance, be it an alibi, rallying the band, or just being a shoulder to lean on.

Stepping out of the diner, Tony felt a newfound determination awakening within him. With Bran's backing and the unshakable bond of The Funk Express, he was ready to confront the brewing tempest of the investigation. In their band, they were not just musicians; they were a family, united by their passion for music and their bond with each other.

And just like a harmonious symphony facing its crescendo, Tony knew that together, they could overcome the dissonance of the present and find their way back to the melody of truth and justice.

Twelve

O'Brien stepped into the quaint bodega, greeted by the familiar tinkle of the entry bell. The shop was a warm mosaic of stocked shelves and the inviting scent of fresh bread and herbs. Nicolás Rodriguez, the proprietor, stood behind the counter, his lean frame and welcoming grin belying the depth of his experience with the neighborhood's changing tides.

"Morning, Nicolás," O'Brien said, a respectful nod accompanying his greeting.

"Detective O'Brien, always a pleasure," Nicolás responded, his voice carrying the gentle lilt of his Hispanic roots. "What brings you to my little corner of the world today?"

Leaning casually against the counter, yet with a keen eye, O'Brien asked, "Nicolás, have you seen Tony Martinez around here recently?"

A softness touched Nicolás's features at Tony's name. "Ah, Tony, yes, he was here yesterday. I've watched him grow up in these streets." His eyes momentarily lost in memories, Nicolás added, "He seemed burdened, like he was carrying the weight of the world on his shoulders."

"Did anything about his visit strike you as out of the ordinary?" O'Brien inquired, observing Nicolás's every expression.

Nicolás paused, thoughtfully rearranging some items on the counter. "Nothing peculiar. He seemed preoccupied, perhaps more with personal matters and his struggles since the band's dissolution. Tony's a kind soul, going through hard times."

O'Brien nodded, mentally cataloging every detail. "Did he mention his plans or where he might go?"

"Just groceries and left. He's a decent young man, Detective. Hard times, but he's remained kind and respectful through it all."

"Appreciate your insights, Nicolás." O'Brien tipped his hat in parting, his mind actively connecting the dots.

Nicolás watched O'Brien leave, concern etching his features. "You don't think Tony's caught up in trouble, do you?"

O'Brien paused; his response measured. "Just tying up loose ends, Nicolás. But keep me posted if you remember anything else."

Stepping back onto the street, O'Brien pondered Nicolás's account. Tony's visit appeared mundane, yet each snippet of information was crucial to the broader investigation. He understood the significance of weaving these fragments into a coherent narrative.

Later, O'Brien delved into police records, seeking any past incidents involving Tony. The search revealed little; Tony's slate was mostly clean, save for a few minor disturbances linked to his band's late-night gigs.

In a dim office, O'Brien briefed the ADA, Kathleen Johnson, a keenly intelligent lawyer known for her meticulous approach. He outlined the facts, culminating with, "I've got a guitar and a torn note. It's circumstantial. I'm considering bringing Tony in."

Johnson, her face a mask of contemplation, replied, "Patrick, this isn't enough for an arrest. We need more solid evidence."

O'Brien's frown deepened. "I agree. Something about this case feels off."

She offered a knowing glance. "Keep investigating, Detective. The truth will surface."

Leaving the office, O'Brien felt the weight pressing down. The city sprawled before him, a labyrinth of untold stories. In this intricate web, finding the truth was a formidable task, but O'Brien was steadfast in his quest for justice. The road ahead was shrouded in uncertainty, yet his resolve was unyielding, fueled by a deep-seated commitment to uncovering the truth.

Thirteen

The Nomad, cloaked in the dim light of his room, poured over the newspaper's bold headline about Natasha's murder. His eyes, icy and methodical, moved line by line, dissecting the article with a predator's precision. It was a goldmine of information, a gateway to a plan long in the making.

The newspaper clippings created a grim tapestry of tragedies and crimes, plastered all around his room. Each clipping was a story, a piece of the intricate puzzle he was meticulously assembling.

Leaning back, The Nomad's thoughts raced. Natasha's death had already stirred the waters, but he envisioned a more sensational aftermath. The temptation to fabricate damning evidence against Tony was strong, but he knew the art of subtlety was key—enough to sow seeds of doubt without being easily debunked.

His hands rifled through his meager possessions, eventually finding some scraps of paper and a well-worn pen. A devious smile crept across his face as he crafted a note, vague yet subtly incriminating. The quality of the forgery was irrelevant; its purpose was to instill uncertainty.

With his scheme laid out, The Nomad ventured out to a decrepit payphone. The phone, while decrepit was still functional, stood with its chipped paint and battered buttons. Dropping coins into the slot, he dialed a number he knew intimately, the phone's gears clattering as the call connected.

His voice, carefully disguised, conveyed a fabricated account to the police. "I saw something suspicious near the crime scene... a figure lurking in the shadows," he intoned, expertly blurring reality and fiction.

After the call, The Nomad felt a surge of triumph. His actions were a catalyst, destined to stir the already turbulent waters of the investigation. He relished the chaos he was masterminding, a spectral manipulator shaping events from the shadows.

Settling back, he basked in the satisfaction of his handiwork. The plot was unfolding, and he had set the stage for the next phase of his grand design. He gazed out at the city, its lights twinkling like distant stars in the night sky. In the drama of Natasha's murder, he was the invisible puppeteer, orchestrating the narrative to his sinister symphony.

Settling back, he basked in the satisfaction of his handiwork. The plot was unfolding, and he had set the stage for the next phase of his grand design. He gazed out at the city, its lights twinkling like distant stars in the night sky. In the drama of Natasha's murder, he was the invisible conductor, orchestrating each movement of this macabre symphony with precise, unseen strokes. Each action he took was like a note played in a complex composition, building towards a crescendo that would engulf Tony and anyone else ensnared in the melody of chaos he was composing.

Fourteen

At her desk in the bustling newsroom of the New York Times, the rhythmic cacophony of typewriters surrounded reporter Julia Steinberg. Known for her dogged persistence and an uncanny knack for sensing the city's heartbeat, Julia had just received an anonymous tip concerning the high-profile Natasha murder case. The caller, their voice deliberately obscured, spoke of a shadowy figure near the crime scene, a detail conspicuously absent from police reports.

Curiosity piqued, Julia dialed Detective Patrick O'Brien, the investigator spearheading the case. The ringing phone sliced through the newsroom's symphony of clacks and chatter.

"Detective O'Brien," answered a voice tinged with a mix of caution and duty.

"Detective, Julia Steinberg from the New York Times," she introduced herself, her tone embodying the confidence of an experienced journalist. "Regarding the Natasha Lopez case, we've received an anonymous lead about an unidentified person near the crime scene. This could be pivotal. Does this align with any aspects of your investigation?"

Pen at the ready, Julia awaited his response, eager to capture any kernel of information.

O'Brien was quick and circumspect in his reply. "Ms. Steinberg, I can't discuss ongoing investigations or unverified leads."

"But the public deserves to know, Detective. Is this angle being pursued?" Julia probed, her journalistic instincts sensing hidden depths.

"I have no comment, Ms. Steinberg," O'Brien reiterated, his tone unyielding.

Persistent, Julia inquired about the boyfriend's rumored involvement, only to be met with the same response. The call ended abruptly, leaving Julia pondering the layers yet to be uncovered.

*****

O'Brien hung up, his thoughts racing. The Times' call was an expected curveball in a high-profile case where rumors and leads were plentiful yet needed vetting.

He picked up the radio to check in with the team surveilling Tony's apartment.

"Car 29, status report," O'Brien requested, his voice a beacon of focus.

"Car 29 here," crackled the response, alert and aware of the case's gravity.

"Update on Martinez's activities today. Any notable encounters or behaviors?" O'Brien's inquiries were sharp, seeking to paint a detailed picture of Tony's day.

"Martinez headed for brunch around 10 AM at his regular spot, on Lexington. Met the drummer from his band. Seemed like a typical catch-up between friends," the officer reported, his voice betraying a reliance on notes.

"What followed?" O'Brien delved deeper, his mind weaving the information together.

"He returned here post-brunch. No departures or visitors since," the officer updated.

O'Brien, deep in thought, instructed continued vigilance, reminding the team to report even the smallest detail.

After the call, O'Brien leaned back, contemplating. In a case where every detail could be a clue, one could not dismiss the seemingly benign brunch with Bran. His role was to comb meticulously through Tony's actions and associations, seeking evidence to build or dismantle the case against him.

In this intricate dance of truth and deception, O'Brien was a key player, navigating carefully through the symphony of clues and leads. Each step he took was akin to a careful note played in a complex composition, where every rhythm and pause held significance. The tip to the Times and the surveillance on Tony were like distinct melodies woven into the larger orchestral piece of the investigation. In this shadow play of fact and conjecture, each of O'Brien's moves resonated like a chord struck in a suspenseful crescendo, with watchful eyes expecting the next harmonious or dissonant note to fall into place in the unfolding mystery.

Fifteen

O'Brien navigated his unmarked car through the crowded streets, his senses acutely aware of the city's symphony: the honking of horns, the distant murmur of conversations, and the faint smell of street food mingling with car exhaust. The skyline, a jagged silhouette against the darkening sky, seemed to mirror his thoughts—sharp and unyielding. His destination was Tony's apartment, a place he had become all too familiar with since Natasha's murder yesterday. The case unfolded in his mind like a complex melody, each note a clue needing to be hit just right to reveal the truth.

Upon arrival, he ascended the worn steps to Tony's apartment, the creaking of old wood under his feet echoing in the dimly lit hallway, its walls faintly stained with years of neglect. A knock on the door, firm and authoritative, broke the silence, resonating with a sense of impending revelation.

Tony answered, his expression a mix of surprise and wariness, his eyes betraying a hint of fear. "Detective, what brings you here?" Tony's voice carried a hint of sarcasm, but the slight tremble betrayed his defensive posture.

"I need to ask you a few more questions, Tony. May I come in?" O'Brien's tone was professional, yet there was an undercurrent of urgency, his eyes scanning Tony's face for any flicker of emotion.

Tony stepped aside, allowing the detective entry. The apartment was sparse, the air stale with the scent of old newspapers and unwashed clothes. O'Brien dove straight to the point. "Tony, do you have a phone in here?"

Tony's brow furrowed; his confusion was genuine. "A phone? No, I had it shut off a couple of months back. Couldn't keep up with the bills." His voice was tinged with embarrassment, a young man struggling to keep his life afloat amid a sea of challenges.

O'Brien's mind raced, his thoughts a whirlwind of possibilities. Tony lacked a phone, so he couldn't have made the anonymous tip to the newspaper. This detail, seemingly insignificant, might clear him of involvement in Natasha's murder.

"Alright, Tony. I just needed to confirm that," O'Brien said, his tone softening. He was already planning his next move—a call to the phone company to verify Tony's statement. This could absolve him, at least temporarily, from suspicion.

Tony watched the detective, a mix of confusion and relief playing across his features, his body language relaxing slightly. "Is that all, Detective?"

"For now, yes. But stay available, Tony. This isn't over yet." O'Brien's words were a reminder of the ongoing nature of the investigation, the relentless pursuit of truth in a city where secrets lay hidden beneath every surface.

As O'Brien left the apartment, the puzzle pieces in his mind rearranged. The lack of a phone connection was a crucial detail, a dissonant note in the melody of the case. In the intricate dance of criminal investigation, especially in a city as complex as New York, assumptions could lead to dead ends. Confirmation from the phone company would be critical. If it proved Tony correct, he might not be The Nomad, and they had to keep working the case, each step a cautious movement in a delicate waltz of justice.

Sixteen

The dawn of the next day brought a clarity that had eluded O'Brien for quite some time. The phone company confirmed to him that Tony's service had been canceled months ago due to non-payment, with no other lines registered for his apartment. This small, yet crucial piece of information shifted the focus of his investigation significantly.

With this new perspective, O'Brien stood once again at Tony's doorstep, intent on delving deeper into his alibis for the other three murders. The detective's mind was a whirlwind of thoughts and theories, each one like a unique fragrance, potent and demanding attention, compelling him to sift through them methodically, either validating or discarding each one.

Stepping into Tony's apartment, O'Brien was immediately struck by the air, heavy with the scent of lingering despair and stale cigarette smoke. He glanced around, noting the sparse furnishings, before focusing his gaze back on Tony. "I need to confirm your whereabouts on specific dates, Tony—Alibis, for the other murders linked to The Nomad. Let's start with June 13th. Where were you?"

Tony leaned against the wall, his expression a mix of recollection and tension. "June 13th, huh?" He paused, his mind rewinding to that day. "I was at a local bar, The Rusty Nail. It's a spot where I sometimes help. I was there the whole night, barkeeping."

O'Brien noted this down, his expression an impassive mask. "Anyone in particular who can vouch for you being there?"

"A couple of regulars and the owner, Mike. He'll remember I was covering for someone that night," Tony replied, his voice carrying a hint of confidence.

O'Brien nodded, making a mental note to follow up. "What about June 22nd?"

Tony shifted; his discomfort was palpable. "That night, I was helping at a charity event. It was a small gig, setting up audio equipment for a local community center." His eyes flickered to O'Brien's, seeking any sign of disbelief.

"And who can confirm that?" O'Brien's voice was steady.

"The event organizer, Mrs. Rivera. She runs the community center. She'll tell you I was there all evening," Tony responded, his voice firmer.

O'Brien's gaze remained fixed. "July 1st. Where were you that night?"

Tony's demeanor changed, his face growing somber. "July 1st..." he trailed off, the memory evidently painful. "I was with Natasha. We spent the entire night at her place. She was my alibi."

O'Brien observed the shift in Tony, the mention of Natasha casting a shadow across his face. "That's going to be harder to verify," he remarked, his voice tinged with a hint of empathy.

Tony looked down, the absence of Natasha hitting him like a wave of cold water. "I know... but it's the truth," he murmured, his voice a faint echo of its former confidence.

O'Brien concluded his questioning with a nod. "Thanks, Tony. We'll be checking these alibis. I'll be in touch."

As the detective jotted down notes, Tony watched him, a knot of anxiety in his stomach. He had told the truth, but how would it look now that Natasha was gone? His mind raced, replaying the nights of the other murders, wishing he had more concrete alibis.

O'Brien seemed lost in thought, his expression a canvas of unreadable emotions. Tony couldn't help but wonder what was going through his mind. Was he still a suspect? The uncertainty was almost unbearable.

Finally, O'Brien looked up. "Thanks for your cooperation, Tony. We'll be in touch if we need anything more." His tone was neutral, but his eyes held a flicker of something unreadable.

*****

As the detective left, Tony felt a cautious sense of relief. From his perspective, it seemed like O'Brien was leaning away from suspecting him as The Nomad. But in a case as complex as this, with so many moving parts, nothing was certain.

The detective's departing figure was a reminder of the ongoing nature of the investigation, a shadow that continued to loom over Tony's life. But for now, at least, it seemed he had distanced himself from the immediate suspicion, a slight reprieve amid the chaos of an unresolved melody, with notes still waiting to be played to their conclusion.

Seventeen

O'Brien found himself in ADA Johnson's office once again, surrounded by the distinctive smell of law books—a mix of leather and paper that spoke of countless cases and legal battles. The ADA sat behind her desk, her expression expectant, eyes sharp and focused.

"I've checked Tony's alibis for the dates of the other murders," O'Brien began, taking a seat across from her. The office's quiet ambiance seemed to amplify his words. "He was at The Rusty Nail bar on June 13th and at a community center event on June 22nd. People there confirmed his presence."

"And the third date?" Johnson's voice was steady, her tone conveying the weight of the decision resting on this information.

"July 1st... that's the problem. His alibi was Lopez, and well, she's the victim," O'Brien said, his voice tinged with frustration. The case's complexity was palpable in the room, almost like a third presence.

ADA Johnson leaned back, the leather of her chair creaking slightly. She tapped a pen against her desk thoughtfully. "This case is becoming more complex by the day, Patrick. I think it's time we bring in some fresh eyes."

O'Brien's eyebrow raised in curiosity. "What do you have in mind?"

"There's a detective, Nancy Schroeder, recently promoted from vice. She's sharp, insightful, and has a knack for seeing things others might miss," Johnson explained, her eyes reflecting strategic thinking. "Having her on this might provide a new perspective."

O'Brien considered this, a mix of relief and apprehension stirring within him. "Nancy Schroeder, you say? I haven't worked with her before."

"She's good, Patrick. Trust me on this. She just wrapped up a complicated vice case with impressive results. I think her fresh approach could be exactly what this investigation needs," Johnson continued, her voice carrying a conviction that seemed to fill the room.

O'Brien nodded, the idea slowly taking root. "Alright, I'm open to it. We could use all the help we can get. When can I meet her?"

"I'll arrange a meeting. Expect her to be up to speed quickly. She's not one to waste time," Johnson said, her hand reaching for the phone to make the arrangements.

As O'Brien left the office, his mind was abuzz with thoughts. The introduction of Detective Schroeder could indeed be the catalyst they needed to break the case wide open. Her background in vice suggested she possessed a unique skill set that might unveil angles he hadn't considered. As he navigated the crowded streets of New York, the city's cacophony a backdrop to his thoughts, he pondered the new dynamics and possibilities this partnership could bring. O'Brien was intrigued to see how Schroeder's addition would harmonize with the rest in the intricate composition of this investigation.

Eighteen

In his cluttered office, maps and stacks of case files, the ambient sounds of the bustling precinct seeping through the walls engulfed Detective O'Brien. His mind was a labyrinth of theories and connections concerning The Nomad murder cases, each path leading to more questions than answers. He waited for Detective Nancy Schroeder, pondering how her insights might illuminate new avenues in the investigation.

The door swung open, and in stepped Nancy Schroeder, a figure new to O'Brien's world. Her entrance was unassuming yet decisive, subtly altering the dynamics of the room. Medium in height, with an athletic build, her physicality spoke of agility and strength honed through demanding police work. Her hair, cut in a practical style, complemented her no-nonsense approach, and her attire—a bright but functional suit—balanced professional decorum and readiness for the unpredictability of detective work. Her face, marked with faint lines, bore witness to her years in vice, where the harsh realities of the city's underbelly were daily encounters. In her gaze was a steely determination, the kind forged in the fires of battling crime and corruption.

She entered the room with measured steps, exuding a quiet yet unmistakable confidence. She commanded attention not through overt displays but through an air of competence and assurance, a testament to her experience in challenging law enforcement situations.

Their eyes met briefly, a silent acknowledgment of mutual respect and understanding passing between them. It was evident that Detective Schroeder was well-equipped to handle the complexities of the case, honed by her time in vice.

"Welcome. I'm Patrick O'Brien," he greeted, extending a hand in a gesture of professional camaraderie.

"Nancy Schroeder. A pleasure to meet you, O'Brien. I've heard this is quite the case," she replied, her handshake firm and assured.

O'Brien gestured to a chair, inviting her to delve into the heart of the matter. "Let's get down to it. So far, we've got a series of murders, all connected to a figure we're calling The Nomad. Tony Martinez, the boyfriend of the latest victim, was our prime suspect, but his alibis check out for two of the three murders."

Schroeder listened intently, her analytical mind absorbing every detail as she scanned the case files handed to her. "And the evidence? What do we have that ties these murders together?"

"We've got a pattern of sorts, locations, and M.O., but nothing solid. No hair or fingerprints, and there's no obvious motive," O'Brien explained, his tone reflecting his frustration.

Leaning forward, her mind already piecing together possibilities, Schroeder posed a critical question. "Seems like you're chasing shadows, O'Brien. What about the possibility of a copycat? Could it be that these murders, although resembling each other, are not linked?

O'Brien pondered her suggestion, his experience in the field reminding him that the improbable was often possible. "It's a stretch, but I've seen stranger things happen in this line of work."

"And Marinez's role in all this? You think he's clean?" she inquired, her eyes still poring over the notes.

"He was with the victim on the night of one murder, and his alibis for the others are solid. Unless he's a criminal mastermind, I doubt he's our guy," O'Brien acknowledged.

Nodding, Schroeder's focus was laser-sharp. "What we need is a fresh angle. Let's revisit the crime scenes and look for overlooked connections or witnesses. Sometimes, the devil is in the details, O'Brien."

Impressed by her acumen, O'Brien leaned back. "Agreed. And let's dig deeper into the victims' backgrounds. There might be a link we're missing."

"Exactly. And what about the community? Street talk, rumors–they can lead us to paths unexplored," Schroeder added, already a step ahead in her thinking.

A smile of respect crossed O'Brien's face. "Seems like we agree, Schroeder. Let's hit the streets and shake some trees."

Nineteen

Tony sat ensconced in a dimly lit corner of a downtown bistro, a place where the clinking of glasses harmonized with the low buzz of conversations. The aroma of rich, savory food mingled with the ever-present scent of city life, a unique fragrance that was unmistakably New York. The bistro had a relaxed, eclectic vibe, adorned with rock posters and an interesting fusion of bohemian and urban styles.

Into this setting walked Nolan Cattervish, known to all as Cat. His entrance was like a page from a fashion magazine dedicated to the legendary David Bowie, whom he emulated with a distinct flair. Slender, with sharp cheekbones and an aura of calm grace, he moved through the bistro as if he belonged to a different, more glamorous world. His eyes, accentuated with a hint of kohl, scanned the room before settling on Tony. With effortless elegance, he slid into the booth, a subtle smile playing on his lips.

Trailing behind Cat was Jacky, the rhythm guitarist for The Funk Express, contrasting with Cat's refined demeanor. Jacky was the embodiment of wild abandon, his long blonde hair a testament to his life's motto, "Fuck the World." His eyes, alive with a fearless and untamed spirit, spoke volumes of a life lived unapologetically on his own terms.

"Tony, man, this is some heavy shit," Jacky said, his voice a rough blend of concern and disbelief as he settled into the booth opposite Tony. He swept his hair back in a gesture that seemed to echo his restless energy.

Cat, the ever-observant, tilted his head, focusing intently on Tony. "Tell us everything, Tony. Start from the beginning."

Tony exhaled deeply; the weight of recent events clear in his eyes. "It started last Tuesday," he began, his voice steady yet filled with underlying emotion. "I was coming home and found Natasha... they murdered her in an alley close to my apartment."

A look of empathy crossed Cat's face, his eyes softening. "God, that's horrific, Tony. I can't even imagine what you're going through..."

Jacky leaned in; his usual brashness replaced by a somber attentiveness. "Who would do something like that to Natasha?"

With a mix of confusion and anger, Tony shook his head. "I don't know. But the worst part is, the cops think I might be involved. They've been grilling me, questioning my every move."

"Those bastards," Jacky growled, his hands balling into fists. "You're one of the good ones, Tony. They're barking up the wrong tree."

Cat spoke up, his voice calm yet assertive. "What's the police's take on this, Tony? Any leads on their end?"

"They're after this character they call The Nomad. There've been other murders, all with a similar M.O.," Tony explained, his hands shivering. "I've been scrambling to prove my alibi for those nights, but it's been a hell of a challenge."

Jacky's expression grew darker. "This is all kinds of messed up, man. You've got to fight this. Prove you're innocent."

Cat nodded, his eyes conveying unwavering support. "We're with you, Tony. Whatever you need, we're here for you. You're not in this alone."

Meeting their gazes, Tony's eyes were a maelstrom of emotion. "This has been a nightmare," he admitted, his voice heavy with the burden of recent days. "I don't even know how to put things back together."

Cat reached across the table, his hand a symbol of unity. "You're not alone in this, Tony. We're here for you, in whatever way you need."

Jacky's demeanor softened, his usual rough edges smoothing out. "We've been through some tough times, but this is different. What's your next move?"

Tony let out a weary sigh, his gaze drifting towards the window where the city lights blurred into a kaleidoscope of neon and shadows. "First step, I need to clear my name. After that... maybe it's time to rethink everything. My music, my life... all of it."

As the night wore on, their conversation wove a tapestry of shared memories, plans, and the stark reality of their current predicament. They recounted poetic tales of past gigs and dreams intermingled with the harsh truths of their present situation, painting a picture of a bond forged in music and resilience.

Twenty

In the shadowed street, where night draped its cloak over the city's ceaseless energy, a figure lurked, unseen yet intensely felt. The Nomad, a ghostly presence in the urban landscape, moved with a stealth shaped by dark intentions. His sharp, calculating eyes fixated on the bistro's inviting glow, where Tony and his former bandmates gathered, blissfully unaware of the malevolent gaze that watched them.

The Nomad's mind, a twisted maze of malice and cunning, peered through the bistro's fogged window. He observed Tony, burdened by recent events that had ensnared him in a web of suspicion and sorrow. Cat and Jacky were there too, living embodiments of a life The Nomad had never known—one marked by camaraderie, music, and a deep sense of belonging.

As laughter and conversation seeped out into the night, The Nomad's thoughts darkened. He fantasized about infiltrating their circle, planting seeds of chaos and fear, not only in Tony's life but also among his friends. Jacky, with his wild spirit and rebellious heart, seemed like an ideal target for his next twisted game.

Veiled by the city's darkness, The Nomad plotted in silence. The city's pulse, with its undercurrents of danger and unpredictability, echoed his sinister intentions.

Peering at Jacky through the bistro's window, he crafted a macabre plan. Jacky was an intriguing challenge, a new piece in The Nomad's grotesque game. He envisioned starting contact with Jacky through cryptic messages, like eerie melodies or fleeting shadows designed to unsettle and sow seeds of paranoia.

As Jacky's discomfort escalated, The Nomad planned to intensify his actions. He would torment Jacky mentally by manipulating his environment—an anonymous phone call in the dead of night, a photograph left in a place only Jacky would discover, each step carefully engineered to push him deeper into a state of fear.

In The Nomad's mind, the final act of this grim drama was taking shape – a climax where he would amplify Jacky's psychological terror to its peak. After methodically dismantling Jacky's grasp on reality, he envisioned a night of heightened horror. In a secluded location known only to the band, The Nomad would enact his final, violent act, extinguishing Jacky's life in a brutal and shocking manner, leaving no doubt about the nightmarish reality.

This act was more than a trap for Jacky; it was a scheme to fracture the group, further isolating Tony. It would sow distress and division, breaking down the support system that Tony relied on, especially in the aftermath of Natasha's murder.

As the night deepened, The Nomad melted away from the bistro, blending into the city's dark fabric. The streets of New York, with their shadowy corners and hushed secrets, served as a perfect playground for his disturbed fantasies. His plans, taking form amid the looming buildings and echoing alleyways, were a symphony of terror he was all too eager to compose.

Twenty-One

Mikhail arrived late, his entrance a subtle blend of nostalgia and the weight of current events. His demeanor, a fusion of somber reflection and subtle excitement, reflected a life deeply entwined with music and the band's rich history. As he stepped into the club, the familiar scent of aged wood and lingering traces of cigarette smoke enveloped him, evoking memories of countless nights spent in this very place. The rough texture of the wooden door handle under his fingers felt like an old friend's handshake.

As he approached Tony, their greetings were brief yet saturated with unspoken empathy, like a melancholic chord resonating between old friends. The ambient sounds of the club—the clinking of glasses, the indistinct murmur of other patrons—formed a dissonant backdrop to their conversation. Mikhail's voice, when he suggested stepping out for air, was a mixture of concern and determination, textured like the raspy timbre of a well-used vinyl record.

In a quieter, more secluded bar, the taste of aged whiskey hung heavily in the air, adding a bitter tang to their conversation. Shadows played across their faces, lending a visual echo to the gravity of their talk. Tony leaned closer; his voice tinged with the sourness of uncertainty. "Mikhail,

I've been thinking a lot lately... about this killer, The Nomad. Should I be the one trying to track him down?"

Mikhail paused, his gaze thoughtful, his hands idly tracing the condensation on his glass, the cool touch grounding him. "It's a heavy burden you're considering, Tony. But it's not just about clearing your name. It's about justice for Natasha, for all those affected by this lunatic."

Tony's face was a canvas of mixed emotions, the bitter aftertaste of his drink mirroring his inner turmoil. "Yeah, you're right. It's just... Where do I even start, Mikhail? This feels bigger than anything I've faced before."

"You start by not facing it alone," Mikhail said firmly, his eyes conveying a deep understanding, his voice as steady as the beat of a drum. "I'm here, and I know this city. We can work through this together. Piece by piece, lead by lead."

Tony exhaled, the tension in his shoulders easing slightly at the touch of Mikhail's hand across the table, a gesture of solidarity. "I appreciate that, Mikhail. It's just so hard to know who to trust anymore. Everyone's a potential suspect."

"Remember, you have people who know you, who believe in you. Lean on that," Mikhail reassured, his voice a steady timbre in the bar's quiet.

A faint smile tugged at the corner of Tony's lips. "Thanks, Mikhail. It means a lot, knowing I've got someone in my corner. I hope we can find anything that leads us to this guy."

"We will, Tony. We'll start with what we know and follow every thread. The Nomad made mistakes; they always do. We'll find them," Mikhail said, his voice unwavering.

Stepping out into the night, the city's rhythm embraced them, a reminder of the ever-present pulse of life around them. Their shared words and plans resonated like a poignant refrain, a symphony of resolve and connection, guiding them through the challenges ahead.

Twenty-Two

In the following days, The Nomad, a phantom woven into the city's bustling tapestry, meticulously shadowed Jacky. Cloaked in anonymity, he observed with the sharp focus of a seasoned predator, cataloging Jacky's movements with chilling precision. The Nomad's plan, a dark crescendo in his symphony of terror, was nearing its peak. He chose his weapon with meticulous care—a thin, razor-sharp garrote wire, as silent and deadly as the night itself, a perfect instrument for his grim task.

As dusk draped the city in a dark veil, the streets whispered quiet secrets, the distant hum of traffic and the occasional footsteps on the pavement creating a soft, rhythmic backdrop. The air carried the faint aroma of rain on concrete, a scent that The Nomad inhaled deeply, feeling it sharpen his focus. In his hands, the garrote wire was cold, its metallic chill seeping into his fingers, a stark contrast to the warmth of the summer night.

Jacky, still lost in the echoes of the music he'd played earlier, approached, blissfully unaware of the lurking danger. The Nomad, emerging from the shadows like a ghost, was intent on his deadly mission. But in a twist of fate, Jacky sensed the danger at the last moment, his intuition like a sudden dissonant note in an otherwise harmonious melody, turning sharply as The Nomad lunged.

The Nomad's surprise at Jacky's reaction disrupted his meticulous plan. A wire, intended to be a quiet and rapid bringer of death, skimmed Jacky's neck and left a sharp cut. The taste of blood, metallic and sharp, filled Jacky's mouth as he fought back with an intensity born of survival. His hands, grappling against The Nomad's, struggled against the wire's deadly embrace.

Their struggle was a cacophony of violence, Jacky's adrenaline surging with a primal beat, lending him strength to match his attacker. He thrashed and kicked, each movement a desperate attempt to escape the suffocating grip of the wire. In the chaos, The Nomad's hood slipped, revealing a face marked by darkness, malice, and a distinctive scar above the left eyebrow—a feature now burned into Jacky's memory.

With a powerful kick, born from the crescendo of his fear and desperation, Jacky loosened The Nomad's grip enough to break free. He stumbled away, gasping for air, each breath a sharp, painful intake, his neck burning with the sting of his wound. His only thought was to escape the suffocating embrace of death.

Stunned by the failure and the risk of exposure, The Nomad disappeared into the shadows, his presence evaporating like a sinister melody fading into the silence of the night. Jacky, left alone and wounded on the quiet street, felt the echoes of their violent encounter dissipate, a chilling counterpoint to the surreal calm that had returned. The memory of the attack, like a discordant note, would haunt him, an ominous reminder of the danger that still lurked in the shadows.

Twenty-Three

In the sterile hospital room, under the rhythmic beeps of monitors punctuating the silence, Jacky lay on the bed, his body a canvas of bruises and bandages. The antiseptic smell of the room, clinical and clean, mingled with the faint, almost out-of-place scent of flowers from a nearby vase, creating a surreal contrast to the stark reality of his condition.

Detectives Harris and Mendez, notebooks in hand, stood around him, their expressions a complex weave of concern, curiosity, and the relentless determination characteristic of seasoned officers. Harris, with lines of experience etched into his face, leaned in closer. His voice, gentle yet probing, was like a cello's deep notes in the quiet room. "Jacky, can you tell us anything more about the attacker? Anything you remember could be critical."

Each inhale was a sharp reminder of the ordeal Jacky had endured, his breaths shallow and painful. Despite the fog of pain and medication clouding his mind, the vivid image of his assailant was etched into his memory. "He had dark hair... and there was this scar right above his left eyebrow," Jacky recounted, his voice a strained whisper, as fragile as the petals of the flowers nearby. "His eyes... they were cold, man. Like there was nothing human behind them."

Mendez, younger and with a keen eagerness in his eyes, scribbled down every detail. His pen scratched on the paper like the faint rustling of leaves. "Did he say anything to you? Any sounds or distinct features about him?"

Jacky shook his head slightly, each movement a symphony of discomfort. "No words. Just the struggle... and the sensation that he relished it." A shiver ran through him, the room's sterile coldness accentuating the memory's chill.

The detectives exchanged a glance, their eyes conveying a silent conversation. This was the first time they had such a detailed description of The Nomad from a survivor. With a subtle nod, Harris signaled Mendez to give Jacky some rest.

As the detectives left, the soft click of the closing door echoed in the quiet space, leaving Jacky enveloped in his thoughts. The hospital room, with its monotonous beeps and hushed murmurs of nurses, became a sanctuary, isolating him from the external chaos.

Jacky's mind wavered between relief and haunting vulnerability. He had escaped death, but the encounter had left indelible marks on both his psyche and body. The weight of his narrow escape loomed over him, an oppressive presence in the otherwise empty room.

Yet amidst this turbulence, a flicker of hope emerged. His survival and testimony might be pivotal in the pursuit of The Nomad, possibly preventing further tragedies. His thoughts drifted to his bandmates, their music a distant, comforting melody. The idea of reuniting with them, of reclaiming the stage, cast a faint light in the enveloping darkness, like a soft, hopeful tune rising amidst a somber symphony.

In the attack's aftermath, as Jacky lay recovering, he understood that his life had veered onto an uncharted path. This chapter of his life, much like a complex and haunting melody, had taken a turn towards a composition that was both sad and hopeful, echoing the resilience and determination that now defined him.

Twenty-Four

The sudden pounding at the door cut through the silence with an urgency that set Tony's heart racing. He swung the door open to find Bran, his face etched with panic and disbelief. "Tony, we need to get to the hospital now. It's Jacky–they have attacked him," Bran gasped, his breaths sharp and uneven, each word infused with alarm.

Tony's response was an instant surge of adrenaline, like a sharp note struck on a piano. Together, they rushed down the stairs and hailed a cab, the urgency hanging thickly in the air. As they sped through New York's streets, the blur of city lights outside the window mirrored the turmoil in Tony's mind, each second stretching like a drawn-out chord in a tense melody.

The hospital's sterile smell and the hushed voices that greeted them created an atmosphere of subdued urgency. Traversing the sterile corridors, they reached Jacky's room, where dim lighting cast a soft glow on his battered form. The sight of Jacky, normally so full of life and energy, now reduced to a vulnerable figure wrapped in bandages, was a harsh dissonance in the symphony of their lives.

"Jacky, man, what happened?" Tony asked, his voice laden with concern and barely concealed fear. He moved closer, his footsteps hesitant, as if afraid of exacerbating Jacky's pain.

Jacky struggled to breathe, with each word a battle against pain. "Walking home... got attacked. He tried to strangle me with a wire," he whispered, his voice as fragile as the quiet in the room.

Bran stood by the door, his fists clenched in barely contained fury, his posture taut with tension. "Did you get a look at him? Who was he?"

Jacky's gaze, though clouded with pain, held a sharp clarity. "Dark hair, scar above the left eye. His eyes... they were like ice. He's 'The Nomad'."

Tony's fists clenched, his jaw tight with a mix of anger and helplessness. "Why us, Jacky? What does this maniac want from us?" His voice was a tumultuous mix of rage and vulnerability, echoing off the walls.

Jacky's fingers gripped Tony's hand, conveying strength and warning. "Be careful, Tony. I think you're his primary target. He's playing some sick game."

The room fell into a heavy silence, broken only by the beeping monitors and the distant sounds of the hospital. Bran, pacing like a caged animal, finally stopped and leaned against the wall, his expression set in a mask of resolve.

"We can't let him keep doing this to us," Tony declared, his voice a blend of determination and fear. He paced the hallway, his movements reflecting his inner turmoil.

Bran nodded, his face hardening with agreement. "We'll find this Nomad and make him pay. We must be vigilant. Dig into every corner of this city."

Tony's voice dropped, laden with worry. "But I might be his next target. What if he comes after me?"

"You won't face him alone, Tony. We're in this together," Bran assured, placing a firm hand on Tony's shoulder. "But stay sharp. This guy is dangerous."

After a moment of heavy silence, Tony spoke with newfound resolve. "We'll face this together. But if something happens to me, keep going. Don't let him win."

Bran met his gaze, his eyes steeling with determination. "You have my word, Tony. We'll end this for Jacky, Natasha, all of us."

As they left the hospital, the city's sounds seemed to echo their grim determination. The challenge ahead was immense, but so was their resolve. The Nomad had brought the battle to their doorstep, and they were ready to fight back. Their synchronized steps on the pavement resonated like a steady drumbeat, ushering them into an uncertain future.

Their lives had transformed into a melancholic symphony, each step a note in a song of resilience and defiance, set against the backdrop of a city that never sleeps.

Twenty-Five

In the bustling precinct, the constant hum of activity echoed the unceasing energy of New York City. Schroeder and O'Brien, surrounded by the clatter of typewriters and the murmur of fellow officers, found themselves at an impasse. The case of The Nomad had stretched their resources and patience thin, transforming the usual cacophony of the precinct into a monotonous soundtrack to their frustration.

As they sat at their desks, surrounded by files and notes, Schroeder's and O'Brien's expressions reflected the weight of the case. The typical sounds of the busy precinct seemed to amplify around them, underscoring the enormity of the task at hand. They exchanged weary glances, a silent acknowledgment of the deadlock they faced. It was clear they needed a breakthrough, a fresh perspective to illuminate the shadowy figure of The Nomad.

Feeling the need for this new angle, Schroeder approached Lieutenant Donaldson, her determination palpable. "Lieutenant, we're hitting a wall with this Nomad case. We need something new, a different approach we haven't tried."

Donaldson, embodying the wisdom and experience of years on the force, pondered her words. "There's an emerging field from the FBI–forensic profiling. It's a new part of their Behavioral Analysis Unit. It might be the fresh approach we need."

Schroeder's eyes sparked with interest, like the first notes of a new melody. "Forensic profiling? That sounds innovative. It's about analyzing the suspect's psychology, right? Their behavioral patterns?"

"Exactly," the lieutenant replied, her voice steady and reassuring. "It's about getting inside the perpetrator's mind, understanding their motives and patterns. This could be the insight we need to catch this elusive predator."

Back at her desk, Schroeder shared this intriguing possibility with O'Brien, who greeted the idea with a mix of skepticism and intrigue. "Forensic profiling? Sounds more like speculative psychology than solid evidence."

Schroeder leaned in; her voice tinged with earnest conviction. "It's more than speculation, O'Brien. It's an in-depth analysis of the criminal mind. Imagine the insights we could gain. This could be our edge in catching The Nomad."

O'Brien, rubbing his neck thoughtfully, conceded to the idea. "Alright, let's give it a shot. But remember, this guy's a ghost; don't expect miracles."

Schroeder's gaze lingered in the distance, her thoughts turning to the future. "One day, when I have more experience, I want to delve deeper into this profiling field. There's something fascinating about unraveling a criminal's psychology. It could revolutionize the way we approach cases."

With a nod of agreement from O'Brien, they initiated contact with the FBI's Behavioral Analysis Unit. This new avenue, exploring the depths of forensic psychology, shone like a hopeful note in the intricate melody of their investigation. It offered a chance to bring light to the dark corners of this elusive case, a fresh rhythm in the symphony of their unyielding pursuit.

Twenty-Six

In the secure, hushed conference room of the FBI's Behavioral Analysis Unit, Schroeder and O'Brien, along with Lieutenant Donaldson, sat across from Agent Jeffrey Jackson, a seasoned expert in forensic psychology. The walls, adorned with charts and maps, whispered tales of unsolved mysteries, while the air was thick with the suspense and tension surrounding the Nomad case.

Schroeder took the lead, her voice a steady cadence, like the first notes of a complex composition, as she outlined the case. "The first crime occurred on the evening of March 21st in an alleyway," she began, detailing each scene, the weapons used, and the victims' profiles with methodical precision. O'Brien, typically a skeptic of profiling, found himself absorbed in the details, his seasoned detective instincts tuning into the rhythm of the narrative. "We believe the perpetrator to be Hispanic, male, in his mid-20s," he added, his gaze shifting thoughtfully to Jackson. "There's no sexual component in the crimes, and the victim selection appears random."

Donaldson added another layer to the melody of their investigation. "The fifth victim survived, providing our first actual description of The Nomad–dark hair, a scar above the left eyebrow, cold eyes."

Agent Jackson, setting down his pen, spoke with the calm authority of a maestro. "A full forensic profile takes time, but I can offer some preliminary insights." He noted the varied nature of the attacks, suggesting a perpetrator who was both impulsive and calculating, a risk-taker yet methodical in his approach.

Schroeder, her interest clearly piqued, leaned in. "Does the variability of the crime scenes and the weapons used show a level of planning despite the brutality?" she inquired; her voice laced with curiosity.

Jackson, tapping his pen in a rhythm that seemed to mirror their thoughts, replied, "It's a paradox. Using opportunistic weapons shows adaptability to the environment. Yet, the execution of the attacks reveals a disturbing level of sophistication and control."

O'Brien, his brow furrowed in concentration, added, "He's meticulous, almost obsessive, in leaving no trace at the crime scenes."

"That level of caution," Agent Jackson responded, "suggests a need for control and power during the crime. The absence of a sexual component, coupled with random victim selection, might point to a deeper, more complex motivation.

The acts themselves may fulfill a need or compulsion, stemming from deep-seated anger or a psychological condition."

Schroeder, tapping her fingers in a silent rhythm, contemplated the insights. "So, we're looking for someone who blends into daily life, maintaining control over their impulses most of the time. But beneath that veneer is a compulsion they can't resist, a darker side that surfaces during these attacks."

Jackson nodded in agreement. "Exactly. To the outside world, they appear ordinary, but this normalcy is a facade, masking intense inner turmoil that drives them to commit these acts."

As the meeting concluded, Schroeder, O'Brien, and Donaldson exchanged glances, their expressions a mix of determination and apprehension. Stepping outside, the surrounding city seemed to resonate with an additional layer of complexity, a hunting ground for a predator they were only beginning to understand. Armed with these new insights, they felt the urgency of their quest to unmask The Nomad before he struck again. Their investigation, like a symphony, had now developed into a more intricate and haunting composition, each revelation a note in the dark melody of their pursuit.

Twenty-Seven

Tony, along with Bran and Mikhail, submerged themselves in the vibrant and diverse bar scene of the city. Night after night, under the lights that cast a warm, golden glow on the streets, they moved methodically from one establishment to another, their determination unwavering despite the crescendo of frustration.

Their journey began in the dimly lit confines of bars like The Rusty Nail, where the air was thick with the scent of stale beer and old stories. Tony, in conversations with seasoned bartenders like Joe and others, sought information with urgency, but each interaction ended in disappointment. Each bartender had their own rhythm and style in the symphony of the city's nightlife, yet none could recall anyone resembling The Nomad.

In venues known for live music, like The Silver Spoon, they found themselves momentarily lost in the melodies of pianists and bands. The music enveloped them, a temporary escape from their quest, yet their inquiries about scarred individuals in their mid-20s remained unanswered. From the rowdy atmosphere of The Hibernian with its live bands to the plush, ambient setting of The Velvet Room, their search yielded only polite apologies and regretful shakes of the head.

The serene backdrop of soft jazz at The Blue Moon Lounge offered a contrast to their mission, yet neither patrons nor bartenders could provide any leads. The Jazz Corner, with its attentive middle-aged bartender, promised to keep an eye out but offered little hope.

Midweek, their search led them to Eddie's, a bustling sports bar alive with the cheers of games, and The Corner Pub, a local haunt where an elderly bartender shared stories but no useful information. The boisterous atmosphere of The Whiskey Barrel and the cozy Irish charm of The Harp were equally unfruitful in their quest for clues about The Nomad.

Venturing into the heart of Brooklyn, at bars like The Brooklyn Dive and The Green Parrot, they were met with indifferent shrugs and blank stares. Even in lively spots like The Underground and the historic McSorley's, their questions about The Nomad disappeared into the void of unanswered mysteries.

Their final stops at Last Call and The Nightingale, known for its late-night crowd, proved no more successful than previous nights. The laughter and music of The Nightingale, a cacophony of joy and celebration, drowned their inquiries, leaving them unnoticed amidst the throng of revelers.

Each night's journey through these myriad establishments painted a vivid portrait of the city's nightlife—a mosaic of sounds, sights, and smells, a symphony of the city's pulse. Yet, the lack of progress in their search cast a somber tone over their efforts, a melancholic melody playing at the edge of hope and despair. They traversed the city's bars like notes on a musical scale, seeking a harmony in their quest that remained just out of reach. Their spirits, though dampened by the silent symphony of the city's secrets, held on to the faint rhythm of hope that somewhere within this urban orchestra, they would find the key to unmasking The Nomad.

Twenty-Eight

In the weeks following Jacky's attack, Tony found himself ensnared in a meticulously orchestrated nightmare, a dark symphony composed by The Nomad. Each day unveiled an additional layer of psychological torment, fraying Tony's nerves, each note of fear pushing him closer to the brink of desperation.

The torment began with cryptic messages. The first, an unmarked envelope on his doormat, contained a note in cut-out magazine letters: "I'm always watching." Tony's heart pounded like a frantic drumbeat against his chest; the message was vague, yet its implications were terrifyingly clear. The constant feeling of being under surveillance left him unnerved, transforming every shadow and passerby into potential threats, his senses heightened to a state of perpetual alertness.

Days later, another chilling note slid under his door: "Remember the past, Tony? It remembers you." These words struck a haunting chord, resurfacing old memories and regrets. The scent of the paper mixed with the bitter taste of fear as Tony read, his hands trembling. The Nomad's precision in targeting his vulnerabilities laid him bare, exposed, his past pains and secrets brutally unearthed.

Tony's sanctuary, his home, turned into a stage for The Nomad's cruel play. The once familiar sounds of his abode now sent him into a state of heightened alertness, every piece of mail a potential threat. The sense of an unseen presence infiltrated and tainted his once peaceful haven.

The psychological assault intensified when "House of the Rising Sun," Tony's favorite song, became a tool of torment. The music, once a source of solace, now unexpectedly played in cafes, on the street, and in bars, transforming a beloved melody into a harbinger of dread. Its familiar chords now carried a taste of fear, turning a cherished tune into a symbol of The Nomad's haunting omnipresence.

A photograph from Tony's childhood, long thought lost, appeared next, adding a deeply personal dimension to the torment. It captured a carefree moment with his late friend Eddie Ortiz, both laughing in the spray of a fire hydrant. The appearance of this photograph was an obvious message: The Nomad had delved deeply into Tony's past, weaponizing sacred memories. The texture of the photo in his hands was a tangible reminder of this invasive intrusion into his personal history.

Each incident unraveled Tony's sense of security. Memories once comforting, attached to the song and the photograph, were now tainted, symbols of The Nomad's invasive reach.

The third week saw The Nomad's manipulation extend to Tony's social circle. Encounters with Joe from The Rusty Nail and others about a man with a scar inquiring about Tony sent shivers down his spine. These accounts transformed every social interaction into a nerve-wracking ordeal; the city's vibrant life morphed into a landscape of potential threats.

The climax of The Nomad's psychological onslaught was a haunting recreation of a past birthday party in Tony's living room. The meticulous attention to detail was unnerving: balloons in specific shades, furniture rearranged to mirror the past, and photographs displayed around the room. The same playlist from that night played softly, each song a sharp stab of lost happiness.

This invasion of his private memories was a profound violation for Tony. Amidst this reconstructed scene, he felt a crushing mix of grief, anger, and violation. His home, once a refuge, now felt like a stage for The Nomad's macabre display.

Day by day, Tony felt increasingly entangled in The Nomad's manipulative web. Paranoia became his relentless shadow, and the vibrant city transformed into a stage for a twisted psychological game. Shadows whispered of danger, and music carried ominous undertones. Once a confident navigator of the city's nightlife, Tony now found himself adrift in a sea of uncertainty, engulfed in the dark, discordant melody crafted by The Nomad.

Twenty-Nine

Fractured by The Nomad's relentless psychological assault, Tony realized he desperately needed Detective O'Brien's help. The pervasive sense of being watched had transformed his once-familiar world into a stage for The Nomad's twisted game, leaving his senses on constant, exhausting alert.

Picking up the phone with trembling hands, Tony dialed O'Brien's number. The line clicked, and O'Brien's gruff voice, laden with the weariness of this endless case, answered, "O'Brien here."

"It's Tony Charisma... uh, Martinez," Tony began, his voice a mixture of urgency and fatigue. "I need to talk to you about The Nomad... he's been... he's been toying with me."

There was a perceptible shift in O'Brien's tone, a note of concern seeping in. "Slow down, Tony. What's happening?"

Tony inhaled deeply, his voice quivering as he recounted the harrowing events. "It started with messages," he choked out, "Notes left at my door... 'I'm always watching,' one said. It's like he's everywhere, all the time."

He paused, a hard swallow echoing his distress. Recalling the notes, a metallic taste of fear invaded his mouth. "Then there was this... recreation of a birthday party in my apartment. My apartment," Tony's voice cracked. "Balloons, cake, pictures... exactly as it was. It was like stepping into a twisted mirror of my past."

Tony shuddered as he described the most intimate violation. "The cake had the same flavor as back then. The sugary sweetness now turned sinister. And the photographs," he continued, his voice trembling, "their eyes seemed to follow me, mocking me with my happiest memories."

With each word, Tony's burden seemed to lighten slightly, though the gravity of his reality remained oppressive. "I can't escape the feeling that he's always one step ahead, turning my life into his playground," he finished, his whisper conveying the depth of his distress.

O'Brien's response carried a serious tone that resonated through the phone. "Tony, you need to stop. You're not a detective. This is dangerous."

"I know, but I can't just sit back," Tony replied, frustration coloring his words. "He's been following me, showing up in places I've been asking about him."

Schroeder's calm, firm voice came on the line. "Tony, we appreciate your efforts, but you're in danger. We'll take it from here. Your information is helpful, though."

Exhaling deeply, Tony ran a hand through his hair, the familiar scent of his aftershave now a reminder of his vulnerability. "Alright. Just... be careful, okay? This guy is like a ghost."

"We will," Schroeder assured him. "Keep a low profile. Let us handle this."

Hanging up, Tony felt a tangle of relief and helplessness. His apartment, once a refuge, now felt like a snare. The shadows played tricks on his eyes, and he moved to the window, peering out at the neon-lit streets of New York. The city's sounds, usually a comforting background hum, now felt distant and alien.

Standing there, Tony recognized the detectives were right, but he was uncertain if he could stop his own pursuit of The Nomad. He had stepped into dangerous waters, unprepared for the depth of the psycho's malice. The fear and paranoia sown by The Nomad hung in the air like a discordant note, a stark reminder of his unintended role in this twisted game. Now, all he could do was wait, hoping for the detectives to bring an end to this nightmare, as the city's rhythm continued outside, a stark contrast to the unnerving silence of his apartment.

Thirty

In the precinct's cramped and cluttered office, Schroeder and O'Brien faced each other, their expressions a complex tapestry of concern and deep contemplation. The constant buzzing of fluorescent lights overhead intertwined with the distant, indistinct chatter of fellow officers, creating a low, continuous soundtrack to their intense deliberations.

"Sounds like our guy is escalating," O'Brien said, his voice tinged with a mix of worry and resolve. "These mind games with Martinez... they're straight out of the playbook the FBI agent described. It's all about control, psychological manipulation."

Schroeder nodded, leaning back as her chair creaked slightly. Her brow furrowed in thought. "Exactly. The profiler emphasized the perpetrator's enjoyment of the power dynamic. These maneuvers with Tony are a deliberate display of dominance, instilling fear."

O'Brien, tapping a rhythmic pattern on his desk, highlighted a significant shift. "But it's different now. The Nomad's previous actions were more physical. This new approach? It's more intricate, more psychological. He's adapting his methods."

Schroeder's fingers brushed over her notepad, her eyes reflecting the gravity of their situation. "It's almost personal with Tony Martinez. Before, the victims seemed random. Now, there's a targeted focus, aligning with the profiler's insights on deep-seated anger or compulsion."

The two detectives sat in a moment of contemplative silence; the weight of their task was palpable in the air. Finally, O'Brien broke the silence, "We need to take this to the lieutenant. If The Nomad's focusing on Martinez, it might be our chance to catch him."

They presented their observations and Tony's account in Donaldson's office, a space filled with the scent of old files and lingering coffee. The lieutenant listened intently, his fingers drumming a thoughtful pattern on his desk.

After a moment, Donaldson spoke, his voice measured and decisive. "So The Nomad's circling Tony now. Risky, but it's a lead."

Schroeder interjected, her voice firm, "A stakeout might be our best bet. Watching Tony's apartment could lead us to The Nomad, or at least some evidence."

Donaldson, the faint smell of his aftershave permeating the small office, considered their proposal and nodded in agreement. "Set it up, but keep it discreet. We can't afford to spook him now."

Back at their desks, Schroeder and O'Brien worked late into the night, orchestrating the stakeout. The precinct gradually quieted down, leaving them enveloped in a cocoon of anticipation, accompanied only by the soft, rhythmic tapping of their keyboards.

Outside, the city hummed with its restless nocturne, oblivious to the intricate drama unfolding within its heart. The coming nights held an air of significance for the detectives, potentially leading them to a face-to-face encounter with the elusive and dangerous Nomad. Their investigation, like a tense and suspenseful melody, reached a pivotal crescendo, one that could change the course of their pursuit entirely.

Thirty-One

Two days later, in the shadowed confines of Lieutenant Donaldson's office, Schroeder and O'Brien sat across from their superior. Donaldson's face, a roadmap of years in service and cases heavy with consequence, carried an expression that melded stern authority with an undertone of regret.

"Schroeder, O'Brien," Donaldson began, his voice resonating with the fatigue of countless battles against the city's darker elements. "I've been in talks with the higher-ups all morning. The media frenzy around The Nomad is intensifying the pressure. They're demanding results, and they want them fast."

Schroeder, usually composed, showed a rare flicker of concern. She leaned forward, her chair emitting a soft creak. "Lieutenant, we've been pushing every angle, using every resource we have. But this guy, he's like a shadow, elusive and unpredictable."

Donaldson exhaled a heavy sigh, laden with the weight of expectations and the unyielding demand for closure. He glanced at the burgeoning pile of case files on his desk. "I know you're giving it your all," he said, his eyes meeting theirs in a brief, shared moment of understanding.

"But our time is running short. The brass gave me an ultimatum: make a breakthrough, or the case goes federal."

O'Brien, his frustration clear, clenched his fist, the sound sharply punctuating the tense atmosphere. "Boss, we're close. The stakeout at Tony's place might be our best chance to draw The Nomad out."

Donaldson nodded slowly; the gravity of the decision apparent. "I understand, O'Brien. But this case has become more than a typical investigation. We're now walking a political tightrope. It's not just about catching a criminal; it's about navigating a complex maze of pressures and expectations."

Schroeder's heart pounded in rhythm with the distant, bustling sounds of the precinct beyond the door. "We can't back down now, Lieutenant. This case has become personal for us. The Nomad is more than just a file."

Donaldson leaned back, his chair protesting under his weight. His gaze softened, recognizing their dedication. "I chose you both for this task for a reason," he said, his voice tinged with sincerity. "But proceed with caution. This guy is cunning and dangerous. And with this ultimatum, the stakes are higher than ever."

As Schroeder and O'Brien stepped back into the precinct, its cacophony immediately enveloped them - the clatter of typewriters, the murmur of conversations, the relentless ringing of phones. An undercurrent of tension flowed through the room, a palpable sense that time was slipping away more rapidly than before.

Outside, the city pulsed to its unending rhythm, unaware of the urgency consuming the detectives. Every face in the crowd, every shadow in the alleyways, could be The Nomad. Schroeder and O'Brien found themselves in a race against time, a tense and suspenseful melody playing against the backdrop of a city that never sleeps. Their pursuit of The Nomad was now a high-stakes concerto, each move a critical note in the unfolding drama.

Thirty-Two

In the precinct, a cauldron of palpable tension, Schroeder and O'Brien grappled with the lieutenant's ultimatum. It hung over them like a tightening noose, trapping them in a vortex of pressure, with stakes higher than ever.

The next couple of days blurred into a continuous stream, each indistinguishable from the next, in a relentless march against time. The precinct's clock ticked steadily, its rhythmic sound a constant undercurrent beneath the perpetual buzz of activity. Desks, cluttered with coffee cups and case files, exuded a mix of stale caffeine and the musty aroma of old paperwork. Officers moved through the space in a choreographed dance of urgency, their footsteps and murmurs blending into a rhythm of determined pursuit.

Outside, the city's cacophony seeped through slightly ajar windows, layering onto the precinct's own. Car horns blared in the distance, sirens wailed intermittently, and the murmur of crowds formed a symphony of urban life pulsating with energy. These sounds, mingled with the soft rustling of leaves and the distant chatter of passersby, mirrored the public's growing anxiety and anticipation.

The city's heartbeat seemed to resonate with collective expectancy, as if every citizen held their breath for news of The Nomad's capture. This symphony, both inside and outside the precinct, provided a soundtrack to the detectives' relentless quest, underscoring the urgency of their mission and the city's watchful gaze.

Schroeder moved through the precinct, each step echoing her mental exhaustion. The air, tinged with the scent of stale coffee and ink, mixed with the aroma of her own frustration. The toll of sleepless nights had dulled her sharpness, and dark circles under her eyes bore witness to the strain.

"Aren't you burning the candle at both ends, Schroeder?" O'Brien's voice, lined with concern, broke through the evening's monotony as they sifted through evidence.

She glanced up, a flicker of a wry smile cutting through her fatigue. "Aren't we all?" she replied. "This case... it's like a shadow over us. Every unturned corner in this city seems to echo with his presence."

O'Brien, massaging his temples where lines of strain had etched deep, agreed. "We're all feeling the heat. We need that breakthrough, and fast. The pressure from the top and the media frenzy are only adding to it."

Schroeder leaned back, her chair creaking under the movement. "It feels like we're chasing a ghost. He's always one step ahead, almost as if he's playing a game with us." She sighed; her gaze fixed on the scattered files. "Every lead, every piece of evidence... it's as if he's expected our every move."

Picking up a file, O'Brien's eyes met hers, reflecting a resolve as firm as her own. "But we can't let up. We have to out-think him, outmaneuver him. We're close; I can feel it."

Schroeder's eyes narrowed in determination. "Right. Let's dive back into the evidence. There has to be a pattern, a clue, something we've overlooked."

Nodding, O'Brien's focus sharpened. "We'll turn this case inside out if necessary. The Nomad's been ahead for too long. It's time we change the game."

As they delved back into their work, the precinct's rhythm continued around them, a relentless, pulsing backdrop to their renewed efforts. In the heart of the city that never sleeps, Schroeder and O'Brien's determination resonated like a solemn yet hopeful note, a counterpoint to the discordant melody of the chase.

Thirty-Three

In the precinct, a cauldron of palpable tension, Schroeder and O'Brien found themselves trapped in a vortex of pressure, their every discussion crackling with an intensity fueled by both personal investment and a tightening noose of expectations.

Days melded into a relentless march against time, indistinguishable from each other. The steady tick of the precinct's clock was a constant undercurrent, punctuating the ever-present buzz of activity. Desks cluttered with coffee cups and overflowing case files carried the scent of stale caffeine and musty paper. Officers moved with a choreographed urgency, their footsteps and murmurs adding to the rhythm of determined pursuit.

"Look at this pattern," Schroeder pointed out, showing a map speckled with colored markers. "Every attack is within a two-mile radius of major transit hubs. He's using the chaos of the city, blending into the crowd after each incident."

O'Brien leaned in; his gaze intense on the map. "Do you remember the vendor's statement near the last crime scene? He saw someone fitting The Nomad's description, but he lost sight of him in the crowd too quickly."

Schroeder flipped through her notebook, finding the relevant page. "And the waitress near the third attack site mentioned a man with a 'predatory gaze' who left abruptly at the sound of sirens. He's always a few steps ahead, watching, planning."

O'Brien's frustration was palpable. "There's no clear connection between the victims, no discernible pattern in his attacks. What's his end game?"

"Could the randomness be the thrill for him?" Schroeder suggested, her eyes weary but sharp. "Or are we missing a link that's right in front of us?"

Leaning back, O'Brien's chair groaned under his weight. "We need to re-examine these witness statements; find the thread we're missing."

The detectives delved back into the evidence, their voices a blend of professional rigor and personal urgency. Each revisited statement and dissected theory brought them closer to understanding The Nomad, their resolve to catch him before he struck again growing stronger.

In the precinct, a hive of activity surrounded them, with colleagues casting sympathetic yet questioning glances. Outside, the media's frenzy only amplified the pressure, reporters circling like vultures for any new information.

Schroeder, ignoring their probing questions, remained focused. Inside, her mind raced against time, the public's fascination with The Nomad palpable in every whispered conversation and shadowed alley.

At night, they staked out Tony's apartment, the weight of their mission a silent companion in the darkness. In these quiet moments, O'Brien pondered aloud, "What's going on in the mind of someone like The Nomad?"

Schroeder, her face half-illuminated by the streetlamps, replied, "Every day, I wonder. What drives him? Is it anger, madness, a need to control?"

O'Brien's gaze was distant, reflective. "There's a calculation in his actions, a game, but we don't know the rules."

Schroeder's eyes followed the quiet street. "It's like he's filling a void with these acts, seeking power in fear."

They sat in contemplative silence, the car's interior echoing their thoughts. The night outside mirrored the darkness of their task, a reminder of the elusive specter they were up against.

Despite the strain and the fraying of their usual camaraderie, a resilient fire burned within Schroeder and O'Brien. Each day, their resolve solidified, a silent pledge to bring The Nomad to justice.

As the city held its breath, the clock ticking into a relentless rhythm, two detectives waged a silent war against the shadows, unyielding in their quest to capture a ghost before it vanished again into the night.

Thirty-Four

In the dim glow of a single bulb, The Nomad sat in his sparse room, a whirlwind of turbulent thoughts and twisted emotions swirling within him. The bare walls, devoid of any decoration, seemed to press in on him, reflecting the oppressive confines of his own mind. He felt himself unraveling, the fabric of his meticulously crafted world coming undone.

What had once been a masterful orchestration of manipulation and control was now turning against him. Each calculated move, every psychological ploy against Tony, had expressed his dominance. But the thrill of the chase was dissipating, replaced by an insidious paranoia.

Pacing restlessly, The Nomad's footsteps echoed in the otherwise silent room. He could sense the detectives closing in, their presence looming ever larger in his psyche. The increased surveillance at Tony's apartment and the intensified police efforts were clear signs that the noose was tightening.

Memories of his past deeds haunted him—the faces of his victims, their expressions of terror and confusion. These memories, once a source of perverse pleasure, now only deepened the void within, resonating hollowly with his descent into madness.

The media frenzy that he had once reveled in now seemed like a taunting specter. The headlines, the speculation, the fear he had instilled in the city—all felt like echoes of a fading dream, a transient moment of triumph slipping away.

In rare moments of clarity, The Nomad recognized his downward spiral. His actions, once calculated and deliberate, were becoming erratic, driven more by desperation than the cold, precise logic that had always guided him.

Seated with trembling hands running through his hair, he felt the walls of his reality closing in. The game that had once thrilled him now felt suffocating. He could almost sense the detectives' breath on his neck, their unyielding pursuit closing in to end his reign of terror.

Yet, surrender was unthinkable to The Nomad. He resolved that if he were to fall, it would be on his terms. His final act, he decided, would be a testament to the chaos he had unleashed, a move that would send shockwaves through the city.

The room grew colder; the shadows deepening as he surrendered to the madness that had claimed him. New York, once his playground, transformed in his mind into the stage for a final, catastrophic act.

Gazing out the window at the city lights, a sinister smile spread across his lips. The endgame was near. The Nomad, the spectral terror of the city, would not fade into obscurity. His finale, a symphony of madness and destruction, would leave an indelible scar on the city's psyche, ensuring his legacy would not be forgotten.

Thirty-Five

Caught in a whirlwind of restless uncertainty, Tony found himself trapped within the confines of his apartment, which had transformed from a refuge into an oppressive cage. The constant buzz of traffic, once a comforting backdrop to New York's relentless rhythm, now served as a relentless reminder of the chaos The Nomad had unleashed in his life.

Days blurred into a monotonous cycle, marked by the sharp taste of black coffee and the stale scent of anxiety. Tony's routines had become hollow motions, leaving him adrift in a fog of indecision. The dilemma of whether to leave the pursuit of The Nomad to the police or continue his personal quest weighed heavily on him, a persistent itch at the back of his mind.

One evening, as the sun set behind the city's skyline, casting a mosaic of shadows across the urban landscape, Tony met with Mikhail in a dimly lit bar. The clinking of glasses and the subdued murmurs of conversations provided a surreal yet soothing backdrop.

"I'm torn, Mikhail," Tony confessed, his voice barely audible over the soft strains of jazz. "I've given everything to O'Brien, but I can't shake this unease. I'm caught in a relentless current, unable to stop searching for him."

Mikhail's face, illuminated by the bar's flickering neon lights, mirrored Tony's turmoil. He leaned in, his voice earnest. "Tony, this chase has pushed you to the edge. Maybe it's time to let the police handle it. They have the resources and expertise we lack."

Tony exhaled deeply; his sigh was nearly lost in the bar's ambient sounds. He ran a hand through his hair, the weariness clear. "I hear you, Mikhail, but stepping back feels like surrender, like letting The Nomad dictate my life. His shadow looms over me, a specter I can't escape."

Mikhail reached across the table, placing a reassuring hand on Tony's. "Continuing on your own is risky. The Nomad is dangerous and unpredictable. We should support the police, not act independently."

Tony gazed out the window at the city lights, feeling both connected to and isolated from the vibrant life outside. "I understand the risks, Mikhail. But I can't just watch from the sidelines. This is personal. I need to end this nightmare."

Mikhail's grip tightened, a silent show of support. "Stepping back isn't defeat, Tony. It's strategizing. We'll find him, but we must do it the right way."

A sudden crash at the bar jolted them back to the present, a stark reminder of the precarious balance in Tony's life.

Outside, the city's lights twinkled like distant stars, a stark contrast to the dim warmth of the bar. Tony's reflection in the glass pondered the same relentless pursuit that consumed him. Turning back to Mikhail, determination flared in his eyes. "I hear you, but I can't step back entirely. We'll work with the police, but I'm not out of this yet."

Mikhail nodded, understanding Tony's resolve. "We'll be strategic. Misdirection could work, but we must keep the police informed."

As they left the bar, stepping into the night's embrace, Tony felt a renewed sense of purpose. The city, with its millions of lights and ceaseless rhythm, seemed to resonate with his determination.

Mikhail clapped Tony on the back as they exited. "We'll get through this together. We'll bring The Nomad to justice, the right way."

Together, they stepped into the night, ready to confront the ghost that haunted them in the heart of a city that never sleeps.

Thirty-Six

Detectives O'Brien and Schroeder, under the growing pressure of the case, embarked on a meticulous reexamination of The Nomad's previous crimes. Driven by the hope that retracing his path of destruction might reveal some overlooked detail or hidden truth, they delved back into the heart of the investigation.

Their first step was to revisit each crime scene. They explored the alleyway, the subway platform, and Central Park, now shrouded in night's shadow. The city's life hummed around them—distant taxi horns and the soft chatter of pedestrians provided a backdrop as they searched for any clue or detail that might illuminate The Nomad's thinking or motives.

Beneath the faint glow of streetlights, O'Brien crouched, his gaze intently scouring the ground. "There might be something we missed, some trace of him," he murmured, examining every inch of the alleyway.

Schroeder, standing with her notebook in hand, mused, "Or maybe there's significance in these places themselves. Some pattern we haven't deciphered." The night air was a tapestry of city smells—a hint of exhaust mingled with the distant aroma of street vendors.

Their second step involved re-interviewing witnesses. They revisited those who had been near the crime scenes or had last seen the victims. Each interview was a delicate dance of questioning, with Schroeder and O'Brien coaxing out any newly surfaced memories or details.

In a cluttered apartment, they had a meeting with a regular of the subway station where they found the second victim. "Can you recall anything unusual that evening, any detail that's come to mind since we last spoke?" Schroeder asked, her tone both gentle and firm.

The woman, fingers wrapped around a steaming mug of tea, hesitated. "I'm not sure... It seemed like just another night. But there was this man, keeping to himself, watching the crowd. Didn't seem significant then..."

The detectives' third step reached beyond their precinct. They consulted with criminal psychology experts, engaging contacts at the FBI and law enforcement agencies in other cities. Each meeting, whether in sterile conference rooms or over static-filled calls, brought a wealth of theories and insights, yet no definitive breakthrough.

Each revisited scene and re-examined statement deepened their understanding of The Nomad. Still, he remained elusive, a specter always just out of reach, making frustration their constant companion in their quest for answers.

As the nights unfolded, with the city pulsing around them, The Nomad remained an enigmatic figure in the vibrant tapestry of urban life. In their unmarked car, staking out another potential lead, O'Brien broke the silence. "We're missing something, Schroeder. He's always a step ahead."

Schroeder, her eyes fixed on the city's lights, felt a mix of resolve and weariness. "We'll find it, whatever it is. We have to," she stated, her voice steady, betraying a hint of fatigue.

Their pursuit of The Nomad was like a complex, haunting melody threading through the dark streets of New York. Each step forward brought them closer to the elusive truth, the crescendo they desperately sought. With unyielding determination set against the nocturnal symphony of the city, they edged ever closer to unraveling the mystery of the man who had cast a shadow of fear over the heart of New York.

Thirty-Seven

In the labyrinthine streets of a city that pulses with unending life, The Nomad moved like a shadow, his new target set on Cat, Tony's close friend and confidant. This pursuit was not just another episode in his cruel game, but a strategic maneuver in a plan meticulously crafted to unravel Tony's psyche, note by note, like a discordant melody in a sinister symphony.

With his mind a tumultuous sea of chaos, The Nomad experienced a perverse thrill in this latest endeavor. Cat was more than just a target; he was a key to inflict maximum emotional turmoil on Tony. The Nomad merged into the city's crowds with predatory grace, shadowing Cat against the backdrop of New York's relentless rhythm and urban cacophony.

He meticulously observed Cat, noting the rhythm of his daily life—the bars he frequented, the paths he walked. There was a sinister precision in The Nomad's stalking, a reflection of his own unraveling sanity. The closer he got to Cat, the deeper he wove himself into Tony's world, feeling a twisted sense of connection.

But mere observation was insufficient for The Nomad. As he had with Tony and Jacky, he began a campaign of subtle yet unnerving intrusions into Cat's life. Cryptic notes appeared mysteriously—under windshield wipers, in mailboxes—each message a silent, watching threat, a discordant note in the growing tension.

Unsettling disturbances followed—misplaced belongings, encounters with strangers who seemed eerily informed, fleeting shadows that danced at the edge of Cat's vision. To Cat, these occurrences were confusing and alarming; to The Nomad, they were deft strokes on a dark canvas he was painting across the city's hidden corners.

In his dismal apartment, The Nomad's thoughts spiraled further into madness. Each orchestrated step offered a fleeting sense of control, a transient satisfaction that quickly dissolved into the void within. He realized he was not so much orchestrating events as his own deranged compulsions ensnared him.

His grip on reality fracturing, The Nomad became increasingly consumed by his alter ego. In fleeting moments of lucidity, he saw his descent into an abyss with no return, yet the compulsion to continue his twisted game was overpowering.

As he plotted his next move against Cat, The Nomad found a dark kinship with New York's shadowy underbelly. The city, with its concealed alleys and faceless crowds, mirrored his fragmented psyche—a place to hide, yet one where he could never escape the ghosts that pursued him.

With each day, as Cat became more entangled in his web, The Nomad's tether to reality frayed further. In his distorted logic, the end justified the means. If isolating Tony meant tearing through the lives of those close to him, then so be it. In the twisted theater of his mind, this was the final act of a tragedy he had authored, a crescendo building to Tony's ultimate unraveling.

Thirty-Eight

In the oppressive confines of his apartment, Tony sat engulfed in solitude, the weight of his world unrelentingly pressing down on him. The walls, once adorned with memories of happier times, now felt like they were closing in on him. Each photograph, each memento, served as a stark reminder of a life that was slipping away, notes of a once-beautiful song fading into obscurity.

His mind had become a battlefield of fear, anger, and a suffocating sense of helplessness. Sleep evaded him, and in its absence, the night's shadows seemed to whisper The Nomad's name, a haunting echo of the psychological siege he was under.

The scars left by The Nomad's manipulations ran deep, unraveling Tony's psyche with each day that passed. The vibrant streets of New York, once a source of life and energy, now felt like a labyrinth of paranoia, every face potentially masking The Nomad's, every sound a foreboding harbinger.

In his fraught interactions with Detectives Schroeder and O'Brien, Tony's desperation was palpable. His voice, often breaking with the strain of fear and determination, and his trembling hands conveyed the urgency of his plight.

"You're not moving fast enough," he would plead, his eyes bloodshot and haunted. "He's still out there, toying with us."

The detectives, trying to balance empathy with their professional duty, struggled to provide solace. "Tony, we're doing everything we can," O'Brien would assert, his voice tinged with a mix of concern and firmness.

But Tony was beyond caution, driven by an overwhelming need to reclaim control from The Nomad. He took risks, venturing into the night, revisiting the paths The Nomad had crossed. In bars, his eyes would scan the crowds, replaying every detail of The Nomad's actions in his mind.

The city's sounds—distant sirens, rhythmic beats from nightclubs, the constant murmur of conversations—became a dissonant soundtrack to his nocturnal quest. He moved through the boroughs like a ghost, a shadow among the living, consumed by an obsession to find his adversary.

Each night deepened his sense of futility. The realization that he was chasing a phantom, always just out of reach, left a bitter taste in his mouth. His once firm resolve was now a wavering flame, threatened by the growing darkness of his situation.

Sometimes, standing on rain-soaked streets, with neon lights reflecting in puddles, Tony felt like an outsider in his own story, powerless against the tide of events pulling him into despair.

Back in his apartment, looking out at the city that never sleeps, Tony faced the grim reality of his predicament. In those moments of quiet, the truth was obvious—he was adrift in a relentless nightmare with no apparent escape.

As days blurred into nights, Tony's life became a grayscale world shadowed by fear and desperation. Walking a thin line between determination and despair, the thought of succumbing to The Nomad was unbearable. Yet, he remained committed to the hunt, even as the shadows grew longer and the faint glimmer of hope dimmed. In the heart of New York, a man was coming undone, his existence unraveling like a melody slowly fading into the silence.

Thirty-Nine

In the dim, flickering light of the precinct's archives, Schroeder sat surrounded by towering stacks of dusty files and the pervasive scent of aged paper. Her attention was riveted on a composite sketch laid before her. Crafted from various witness descriptions, the face in the sketch was both hauntingly familiar and frustratingly elusive, reminiscent of a melody half-remembered yet slipping away.

Beside her, O'Brien sifted through old case files, the rustle of paper echoing in the quiet room. The weight of the lieutenant's deadline cast a shadow in the already cramped space.

"Schroeder, look at this," O'Brien interrupted the silence, his voice urgent. He handed her a weathered file with frayed edges and yellowed pages. As Schroeder opened the file, a musty scent wafted up. The report detailed a disturbing assault on a city bus years ago by an individual with a history of mental instability. A surge of disbelief washed over her upon hearing the suspect's description: piercing eyes, a recognizable scar above the left eye— features remarkably similar to the sketch of The Nomad.

The file contained grainy photos and a detailed account of the attack. Martha Sullivan, the victim, was attacked with no justification. The authorities apprehended the suspect, Arthur Hitchens, but later released him because of mental health concerns, with no records of subsequent institutionalization. They observed his erratic behavior during interrogation - he was lucid sometimes and unsettlingly out-bursting at others.

Schroeder scanned the file, a realization dawning. The suspect's profile aligned eerily with their current investigation. "Arthur Hitchens," she murmured. "Could he have developed into The Nomad?"

O'Brien leaned in, somber. "It's possible. People change, especially with his background. This could be the breakthrough we need."

Their discovery cast a new light on the investigation. The possibility that their elusive Nomad was a man with a troubled past and a known history of violence added a chilling dimension to their search.

Further investigation led them to another key discovery. In the archives' dim light, they examined photocopied handwriting samples from unsolved cases of the past decade. Among them was a ransom note from an unsolved disappearance—Emily Caldwell.

"This could be it," Schroeder whispered, noticing similarities in the handwriting. But her mind was elsewhere;

she had known Emily years ago. This personal connection, long-forgotten, now resurfaced with startling clarity.

O'Brien, focused on the handwriting, missed the recognition in Schroeder's eyes. "How does Emily Caldwell's disappearance connect to The Nomad?" he pondered.

Schroeder, composing herself, replied, "We need to dig deeper into this. There's a link here we're missing."

Their next revelation sent a shiver through them. A previous victim, thought to be a ballet dancer, was actually a stripper at a downtown club—a club where Arthur Hitchens had worked as a bouncer.

"This changes everything," Schroeder said, a new angle of their investigation coming into view. "It's not random violence. It's personal."

O'Brien rubbed his chin thoughtfully. "If Hitchens is our guy, he's targeting people from his past. It's like he's unraveling."

Determined to follow this new lead, they prepared to visit the club, venturing into a part of the city they seldom explored. The seedy underbelly of New York, with its dim lights and heavy air, held a tangible lead in their hunt for The Nomad.

As Schroeder and O'Brien delved deeper into this new connection, the pieces of the puzzle began forming a clearer, yet increasingly complex and disturbing picture of The Nomad and his possible identity as Arthur Hitchens.

Forty

In Lieutenant Donaldson's office, the air crackled with a renewed sense of urgency. Schroeder and O'Brien laid out their latest discoveries: the composite sketch of Arthur Hitchens, the striking handwriting similarities, and the unexpected link to the stripper. Each piece of evidence added gravity to their argument, like distinct notes in an increasingly complex melody.

Donaldson, leaning forward in his chair, surveyed the sketch and documents with a discerning eye. The faint aroma of his coffee mingled with the musty room air. "Impressive work, but Hitchens is like a phantom—no known address, no recent sightings," he noted, his voice reflecting the weight of their challenge.

Schroeder, her mind abuzz with potential strategies, suggested, "If we release his name and sketch to the media, we could enlist the public's help. It might just corner him."

O'Brien, thoughtful and cautious, countered, "But broadcasting his identity is risky. It could drive him deeper underground or provoke unpredictable actions."

The room fell silent, the weight of their decision palpable. Outside, the gentle buzz of the precinct was a distant backdrop to the intensity within the office.

Donaldson acknowledged the risks, "We're not just dealing with a criminal—Hitchens is elusive, a master at evading capture. We need to be strategic."

Schroeder, determined, added, "Taking this chance could close the net around him. It's a risk that might be necessary."

O'Brien exhaled, the tension in his stance evident. "We'll proceed with caution. But we must prepare for every outcome."

The decision to publicize Hitchens' identity hung in the air, charged with potential yet fraught with danger. The lieutenant's voice broke the silence, "Proceed, but tread carefully. Hitchens is unpredictable, and we're running out of time."

Schroeder nodded, her resolve clear. "I'll draft a press release immediately. We'll be vague on details, giving Hitchens no advantage."

O'Brien, acknowledging the gravity of their course of action, sighed, "It's risky, but I'm on board. We need to be ready for any backlash."

The lieutenant leaned back, his chair creaking. "Keep me informed on every development. We can't afford any missteps now."

As they exited the office, the familiar precinct sounds—the chatter of officers, the rhythmic typing, the occasional phone ring—greeted them. Yet, an undercurrent of anticipation ran beneath this everyday symphony, as if the precinct itself was holding its breath.

The pursuit of Arthur Hitchens, possibly The Nomad, was entering a crucial phase against the backdrop of New York City's vibrant life. For Schroeder and O'Brien, the next steps were a tightrope walk, with the city's—and potentially The Nomad's—eyes on their every move.

Beyond the precinct walls, New York continued its relentless rhythm, oblivious to the pivotal shift in its unfolding story. But soon, the name Arthur Hitchens would dominate conversations, as the city's hidden corners revealed their most sinister secret.

Forty-One

For Detective Nancy Schroeder, the pursuit of The Nomad had transformed into a deeply personal odyssey. As she thumbed through Emily Caldwell's yellowed case file, a deluge of memories, long submerged under the weight of time and duty, resurfaced with poignant clarity. Emily wasn't just a name in a cold case file; she was a chapter from Schroeder's college days, a time of first love and youthful innocence, leaving an indelible mark on her heart.

Seated at her desk in the precinct, surrounded by the musty scent of old records, Schroeder found herself enveloped in vivid recollections. The sterile buzz of the fluorescent lights above flickered, seemingly in tune with her tumultuous thoughts, casting a harsh light on the sea of forgotten faces and unsolved mysteries sprawled before her.

The sound of Emily's laughter echoed in her mind, a melody that had once filled her days with joy. She remembered the sparkle in Emily's eyes, brimming with dreams and aspirations, and the gentle warmth of her touch, now a wistful memory. These once-sweet remembrances now bore the weight of loss and unanswered questions. The potential link between Emily's unsolved disappearance and

The Nomad intertwined sorrow, guilt, and a relentless desire for closure.

O'Brien, perceptive as always, noticed the subtle change in Schroeder's demeanor. "Schroeder, is everything alright? You seem... distant," he inquired, his voice laced with concern.

Jolted back to reality, Schroeder swiftly masked her inner turmoil. "I'm fine, O'Brien. Just deep in thought about the case," she responded, her voice steady but masking the emotional storm within.

As the investigation intensified, the ghost of Emily haunted Schroeder. Her mind often wandered back to their shared moments. Each clue and piece of evidence they unearthed felt like a step not only towards capturing The Nomad but also towards resolving the shadows of her past.

Nights became restless, filled with dreams where Emily's silhouette merged with whispered names. Schroeder would walk the streets of the city, the city's pulse mirroring her solitude. The flickering neon signs in the night, like distant beacons, became poignant reminders of a love lost to time.

Driven by more than her duty as a detective, Schroeder's pursuit of The Nomad intertwined with her need for personal closure. Emily's memory, lingering like a half-forgotten song, demanded the truth.

The case had evolved into a journey through both The Nomad's twisted path and her own buried history. Each step in the investigation led her deeper into her past, a path veiled in the shadows of what might have been.

Schroeder, more than a name on the precinct's roster, had become entwined in a narrative bridging her past and present. In chasing The Nomad, she was also chasing echoes of her own history, seeking answers in a case that resonated as deeply within her as the rhythm of her own heartbeat.

Forty-Two

O'Brien sat in the unmarked car, the hum of the engine blending with the distant rhythm of New York City. Across the street, his gaze was fixed on Tony's apartment building, where he had set up his nightly vigil. The bitter taste of lukewarm coffee and the rhythmic tapping of his fingers on the steering wheel marked the passage of time.

Surrounded by the symphony of the city—distant car horns and muffled voices of night dwellers—O'Brien's focus never wavered from the task at hand. Every piece of evidence and lead they had gathered seemed to bring them closer to catching The Nomad, yet the elusive figure remained a step ahead, a phantom in the shadows of the city.

A seasoned detective's instinct told him they were on the verge of a breakthrough. O'Brien's eyes scoured the street, analyzing every movement, every passerby in the night's obscurity.

Suddenly, a figure emerging from a nearby alley caught his attention. The man's gait, his build, his manner of moving—O'Brien's pulse quickened. Could this be The Nomad?

Without hesitation, O'Brien was out of the car, his hand in his holster. He followed the figure stealthily, his every sense heightened, the sounds of the city fading into the background.

As he turned a corner, O'Brien found himself face-to-face with the man he had been pursuing. The Nomad stood there, his eyes cold and emotionless, a sinister smile playing on his lips.

"Detective O'Brien," The Nomad's voice was a sinister whisper. "We meet at last."

O'Brien drew his weapon, his voice firm despite the tension. "Arthur Hitchens, you're under arrest for the murders of-"

Before he could finish, The Nomad lunged, a blade glinting in his hand. The alleyway transformed into a battleground, lit only by the faint light of a flickering streetlamp. O'Brien's heart pounded fiercely, a mix of fear and determination fueling his actions.

The struggle was intense, a violent dance in the shadowy confines of the alley. O'Brien thought of the victims, each move fueled by a resolve to bring The Nomad to justice.

A gunshot shattered the night's stillness. The Nomad staggered back; disbelief etched on his face. O'Brien had struck his target, but the victory was fleeting.

With a last surge of fury, The Nomad retaliated, his blade finding its mark. O'Brien felt a sharp pain, his strength waning rapidly.

He collapsed, the cold concrete of the alley floor beneath him. Gazing up at the narrow slice of sky above, his vision blurred, his mind overwhelmed with emotions—regret, a sense of injustice, and thoughts of his colleagues, the case still unresolved.

As The Nomad disappeared into the night, O'Brien lay there, his life ebbing away. His final thoughts were of the pursuit of justice, the realization that his fight was ending.

The night enveloped him, the distant sounds of the city fading into a solemn lullaby. Detective Patrick O'Brien, in his last stand for justice, succumbed to the darkness, his final breath a silent testament in the city that never sleeps.

Forty-Three

The one known as Arthur Hitchens, identified to the city as The Nomad, staggered as he navigated the back alleys of New York, clutching his injured left shoulder. The wound, a result of Detective O'Brien's gunshot, pulsated with intense pain, a burning reminder of his narrow escape from death.

Seeking refuge, he entered an old, abandoned building nestled in the city's heart. The musty air of the forsaken structure filled his nostrils, contrasting with the crisp night air outside. Each movement sent waves of excruciating pain through his body, starkly underscoring his vulnerability.

In the dim light filtering through broken windows, Hitchens attempted to dress his wound, his thoughts replaying the confrontation with O'Brien. He recognized a formidable foe in the detective, a reflection of his own tenacity. Yet, he saw something deeper in O'Brien's eyes—a personal drive that went beyond duty, unsettling Hitchens.

This realization left him unnerved. O'Brien had become more than a pursuer; he was an integral part of the narrative Hitchens had woven. Although necessary for survival, O'Brien's death left a void, an echoing hollowness within Hitchens.

He looked at his blood-stained hands, stark reminders of the path he had chosen. This visceral representation of his actions led him to a lonely and painful moment of reckoning.

As he crudely bandaged his wound, the pain was relentless, a physical torment mirroring his deeper inner affliction. The adrenaline rush of the chase, once exhilarating, had faded, leaving him with a bitter realization of his reality. Hitchens had become the embodiment of the darkness he once sought to outmaneuver, now a hunted shadow.

Throughout the night, Hitchens wrestled with his thoughts in the building's silence, the surrounding desolation amplifying his inner conflict. Outside, New York continued its unending rhythm, but within these decaying walls, Hitchens faced his desolation.

Detective O'Brien's death marked a pivotal point, a threshold crossed from which there was no return. The Nomad recognized his story was drawing to its conclusion, the final act of a tragedy he had authored.

The pain from his shoulder resonated like a dissonant chord, a relentless physical reminder of his mortality. Yet, it was the anguish within his soul that was most excruciating, a crescendo of inner turmoil overshadowing his physical suffering.

In the shadows of the city, The Nomad, escaping the identity of Arthur Hitchins, confronted the depths of his own darkness. Wounded in body and spirit, he found himself ensnared in a tragic symphony of his own making, a man caught in the relentless grip of his twisted fate.

Forty-Four

Schroeder sat motionless in Lieutenant Donaldson's office, the reality of O'Brien's fate echoing in her mind like a mournful refrain of a sad song. "O'Brien's gone, Schroeder. He confronted The Nomad. There was a struggle... he didn't make it," Donaldson's words resonated, distant and surreal. O'Brien, her steadfast partner in their relentless pursuit of justice, was now just a memory. The stark realization of his absence hit her like a physical blow, shattering her sense of reality.

It enveloped her in a whirlwind of grief, anger, and disbelief. The precinct, usually a hub of activity and order, now felt distant, its vitality dimmed in the shadow of O'Brien's demise.

Donaldson's hand on her shoulder was a gentle anchor in the tempest of her emotions, but Schroeder felt adrift, lost in a sea of memories and unrealized possibilities. She remembered the late nights working on the case with O'Brien, their shared moments of laughter amidst the chaos, and the unspoken bond that had formed between them.

Donaldson's voice broke through her thoughts, tinged with concern. "Take some time, Schroeder. Go home. Rest."

Rising from her chair, Schroeder's movements felt disconnected, as if she were observing herself from afar. The precinct corridors, once pathways of purpose, now appeared as endless tunnels of shadow. Her colleagues' faces blurred past her, their words of condolence barely registering.

Stepping out into the street, the city continued its relentless pace, indifferent to her personal upheaval. The setting sun cast long, somber shadows on the pavement, adding to the melancholic atmosphere. The everyday symphony of the city—the blare of horns, the murmurs of the crowd—seemed distant and insignificant, a stark contrast to the void within her.

Walking aimlessly, the weight of O'Brien's death felt like a suffocating cloak. The city's vibrant life, which had once been part of her, now seemed alien, leaving her feeling like a specter in a once-familiar world.

Amidst her grief, one thought pierced through with unwavering clarity—The Nomad. The cause of her anguish, the one who had taken O'Brien's life. A new resolve formed within her grief.

Silently, Schroeder made a vow—to O'Brien, to Emily, to herself—that she would bring The Nomad to justice. It was a promise born from sorrow, a commitment to honor her fallen partner.

As night enveloped the city, its lights flickered against the darkness like distant stars. Schroeder moved through the streets, transformed by loss, driven by a renewed purpose. Her pursuit of The Nomad had become more than a case; it was a personal crusade, a quest forged from loss and fueled by the memory of O'Brien.

Forty-Five

Schroeder returned to the precinct, her heart a whirlwind of grief and unwavering resolve. The familiar hum of police work within the precinct walls now felt subdued, its vibrancy dimming against the storm of emotions within her.

With purposeful steps, she made her way to Lieutenant Donaldson's office. The usual comforting sounds of the precinct—the rhythmic tapping of keyboards, the internal tempest she was navigating overshadowed the subdued murmur of conversations.

Entering Donaldson's office, the gravity in his expression signaled a significant shift in her journey. "Schroeder, have a seat," he said gravely, but she was already bracing for unwelcome news.

"There's no time to sit, Lieutenant. We need to intensify our pursuit of The Nomad," Schroeder responded, her voice a blend of urgency and raw emotion.

Donaldson sighed, meeting her gaze. "I'm sorry, Schroeder, but you're being reassigned. You're off the Nomad case."

The words hit Schroeder like a tidal wave, disbelief and indignation flooding her senses. "Reassigned? After O'Brien's sacrifice? I need to see this through!"

"The higher-ups are concerned about your closeness to the case. They view it as a liability," Donaldson explained, sympathetic yet unwavering.

Frustration surged within Schroeder, her dedication to the case fueling her defiance. "My connection to this case is precisely why I need to be the one to finish it."

Donaldson remained firm. "Your state of mind is a concern. It's affecting your judgment."

"I can't just step back. Not now," Schroeder countered, her resolve unyielding.

Donaldson stood, signifying the finality of the decision. "You're on leave, effective immediately. It's time to process O'Brien's loss."

But Schroeder's mission transcended departmental rules. "I'll process it by catching The Nomad. Badge or no badge."

"If you go rogue, you'll be off the force," Donaldson cautioned, regret lacing his words. "Hand in your badge and gun."

Schroeder met his gaze steadily. "If that's the price." She placed her badge and gun on his desk, leaving behind her official role.

Exiting the office, the precinct's atmosphere was tense, her colleagues' expressions a mix of respect and concern. The precinct's familiar sounds faded, overshadowed by her singular focus.

Stepping onto New York's streets, Schroeder felt isolated, yet driven by a powerful purpose. The city's landscape became the backdrop for her solo mission.

She moved through the urban sprawl, her solitary figure casting a determined shadow against the concrete and steel. Fueled by loss and resolve, Schroeder embarked on her lone quest to bring The Nomad to justice.

Her path, though detached from her official capacity, was driven by a profound personal commitment. It was a mission echoing with the intensity of a heartfelt, mournful ballad, as personal as it was professional. In the city that never sleeps, Detective Nancy Schroeder, now unbound by her badge, pursued a quest that resonated deeply with her own story of loss and determination.

Forty-Six

Early morning draped New York City in a shroud of shadows and muted lights, its vast streets transforming into a domain where darkness' reign was fleeting. In this obscured labyrinth, The Nomad, propelled by a blend of pain and malevolence, plotted his most sinister scheme yet. His shoulder, wounded by O'Brien's bullet, throbbed relentlessly, a painful reminder of his vulnerability.

He targeted Nolan 'Cat' Cattervish, a pivotal figure in Tony's life. Despite the agony radiating from his shoulder, The Nomad ambushed Cat with a predator's precision in the shadowy street, leveraging the surprise of the dwindling night.

Cat, surprised, tried to fend off the attack. But The Nomad's ferocity, fueled by desperation, overwhelmed him. "What do you want?" Cat cried, struggling in vain.

"Quiet," hissed The Nomad, his voice a blend of pain and spite. "You're a message for Tony." With a ruthless strike, he knocked Cat unconscious, his own wound reopening.

Dragging Cat to an abandoned building was a torturous endeavor, each step a battle against his pain. In a desolate room, illuminated by a flickering candle, The

Nomad secured Cat with heavy chains, the clank of metal echoing off barren walls.

As Cat regained consciousness, his eyes reflected fear and confusion. "You're mad," he accused, straining against his bonds.

The Nomad, looming over him, retorted, "Madness is a matter of perspective. You're a symbol, Cat. A piece in the game with Tony."

Cat's defiance was palpable. "You think this will bring him to you?"

The Nomad leaned closer. "Oh, he will come. He understands the stakes."

"You won't get away with this," Cat declared, but The Nomad's laugh was cold and humorless.

"I want him to find me," he replied. "It's the climax of our drama. You are the key to the final showdown."

The Nomad crafted a cryptic note to lure Tony, a puzzle embedded with references only Tony could decipher. The note was a weaving of their shared past and Cat's predicament.

Tony-

In the shadows of our past, a familiar feline face lies bound by chains of the present. Follow the trail of memories we share, to the place where light and darkness meet. Your search ends, and another begins. Time is ticking, and the night grows weary.

He slipped the note under Tony's apartment mat with stealth, leaving no trace but the ominous message.

As The Nomad retreated into the city's anonymity, the pain from his wound a constant companion, he felt a grim satisfaction. The stage was set, the players positioned, and the final act of his grand design was imminent.

Retreating into the shadows, his wound bleeding through the bandage, The Nomad's once ordered mind now mirrored the decaying buildings around him. Cat, shackled in the dim room, was more than a captive; he was a symbol of The Nomad's chaotic descent, a pawn in a game that had spiraled out of control.

As morning light tried to pierce the gloom of the forsaken building, the only sounds were the city's distant hum and Cat's labored breathing. In that shadowed room, The Nomad, his pain and madness converging, awaited the ultimate confrontation with Tony, a dark prelude to their inevitable clash

Forty-Seven

Evening shadows spread across New York City, elongating its contours, as Tony arrived back at his apartment. The city's relentless pulse stood in stark contrast to the maelstrom of emotions raging within him. His mind was a turbulent sea, dominated by thoughts of The Nomad and the perilous game that was unfolding.

At his doorstep, an out-of-place piece of paper captured his attention, an intentional anomaly against the ordinary backdrop of his entrance. A surge of dread, simmering within him all day, intensified as he picked up the note.

Tony's eyes darted across the message, each word striking a discordant chord in the ongoing ordeal. His heart pounded like a relentless drum, the message from The Nomad resonating deeply. The implication was crystal clear—Cat, his trusted friend, was in danger, now a pawn in The Nomad's twisted game.

A whirlwind of fear, anger, and guilt engulfed Tony. The realization that The Nomad was targeting those closest to him struck a deep emotional chord. Overwhelmed by the guilt of putting Cat in danger, Tony grappled with the weight of each decision in this deadly game, which had now breached into his personal life.

Clutching the crumpled note, Tony's mind raced to decipher The Nomad's cryptic words. "Shadows of our past... where light and darkness merge." The riddle, woven into their shared history, echoed in his thoughts.

With a mix of resolve and caution, Tony re-emerged into the night. New York's familiar streets now appeared as a labyrinth, each twist and turn laden with clues, each passerby a potential link in The Nomad's narrative.

Tony navigated with deliberate precision, transforming his usual impulsive nature into focused determination. He revisited key places, searching for any clue that might lead him to Cat.

The weight of responsibility pressed heavily on him, each ticking minute stretching into an eternity. The city's vibrant lights and cacophony formed a stark backdrop to the urgency of his quest.

As the night deepened, so did Tony's concern for Cat's safety. Aware of The Nomad's cunning and ruthlessness, he knew that any error could be catastrophic. Yet, amid the fear, a steadfast determination to outwit The Nomad and save Cat ignited within him.

In the city's icy embrace, shadowed by uncertainty, Tony pressed on, fueled by a potent mix of fear and resolve. The Nomad's note was more than just words; it was a challenge, a duel of intellects with the highest stakes. Amid this storm, Tony recognized the necessity to confront this challenge directly, for Cat's sake and his own.

Forty-Eight

The crisp night air of the city, tinged with the faint scent of rain on concrete, was alive with the city's characteristic hum—a symphony of urban life that enveloped Tony and Bran as they navigated through the streets. Their quest to find Cat and The Nomad had taken them through a labyrinth of memories and familiar haunts, the aroma of street food mingling with the exhaust of passing cars. Yet as the night progressed, their efforts seemed increasingly fruitless, adding layers of frustration and anxiety to Tony's already burdened psyche.

Turning down a seldom-used alley, a shortcut known only to those with a history in these parts, a creeping sense of unease escalated within Tony. The alley's shadows loomed ominously, elongating and distorting in the dim light, creating an otherworldly realm where the vibrant sounds of the city seemed distant, muffled as if behind a veil. Tony's footsteps echoed on the cobblestone, each step resonating with his growing apprehension.

This eerie quietude shattered abruptly when two figures, shadows themselves, emerged with predatory swiftness. The scant light did little to reveal their features, but their hostile intent was unmistakable. Bran, caught off-guard, could barely register his shock before the larger assailant pounced. The attacker, a hulking silhouette of menace, moved with a dangerous fluidity, his hands reaching out to ensnare Bran. With a swift motion, he slammed Bran against the wall, where graffiti whispered tales of the alley's past. The thud of Bran's body hitting the wall resonated through the alley, a grim counterpoint to the usual city sounds.

"Stay silent," the attacker hissed, his breath a noxious mix of stale tobacco and something more sinister. His words carried an undeniable threat, his grip on Bran's collar both unyielding and punishing.

Meanwhile, Tony, momentarily paralyzed by the suddenness of the ambush, faced the second attacker. This one was leaner, his movements imbued with a calculated, deadly precision. Tony's instincts screamed a warning, but before he could react, the attacker struck with chilling expertise. Tony doubled over as a sharp pain erupted in his abdomen, a brutal reminder of his vulnerability. The impact forced the air from his lungs in a gasp, and waves of agony radiated outward, clouding his senses. He clutched at his stomach, struggling against the overwhelming pain.

Blurred shadows danced around Tony as he fought to maintain consciousness. He could barely discern the silhouette of his assailant, a figure merging back into the darkness from which he had come, a stark reminder that this was no ordinary street crime.

Leaning in, the assailant's voice slithered into Tony's ear, a venomous whisper. "Consider this a warning, Charisma. Abandon your hunt. Any further pursuit will bring consequences beyond your worst nightmares."

"Who sent you?" Tony gasped, defiance lacing his pained voice despite his compromised state.

The mugger's laughter was a cold, humorless sound. "Think of me as a concerned observer. Remember, Charisma, step back while you still have the chance."

As quickly as they had appeared, the attackers dissolved back into the alley's shadows. Bran, released from his assailant's grasp, hurried to aid Tony. "Tony, talk to me. Are you okay?" Bran's voice was thick with worry and confusion.

On the ground, a clue: a wallet, likely dropped in the scuffle. Tony, pain etched on his face, picked it up. "This could be a lead," he said, hope flickering in his eyes despite his agony. Inside, among the usual contents, was a photograph–a young woman, her image worn and personal, evoking a sense of curiosity in Tony.

The violent encounter, though harrowing, had inadvertently provided a potential clue. The contents of the wallet, particularly the photograph, might just unravel the identity of at least one assailant, and perhaps their connection to The Nomad.

Bran, his expression marked by deep concern, helped Tony to his feet. "We need to get you to a doctor, Tony. That hit looked bad."

Holding the wallet, Tony shook his head negatively, his resolve undiminished by the physical pain. The assault was a clear escalation, a tangible threat from the shadows. But it had only fortified Tony's determination. Intimidation or violence would not deter him. He would find Cat, confront The Nomad, and seek justice, whatever the cost.

Exiting the alley, Tony and Bran stepped back into the sprawling tapestry of the neighborhood. Tony, though battered and bruised, was resolute, his determination undiminished. He rejoined the urban flow, a man on a mission, moving to the rhythm of a city that hummed with both danger and possibility. Like a somber melody weaving through a complex symphony, Tony's resolve played against the backdrop of the city's vibrant life, his quest for justice harmonizing with the ceaseless beat of the streets.

Forty-Nine

The morning sun filtered through Tony's curtains, casting elongated, melancholic shadows across his apartment, a visual echo of his heavy heart. The remnants of the previous night's chaos—the brutal attack, the enigmatic note, and Cat's abduction—weighed oppressively on him. Nursing his bruised abdomen, Tony knew acutely that time was of the essence. He needed to connect with Detective O'Brien.

Feeling the urgency pulse through him, Tony hastily left his apartment and headed to the nearby bodega, where a pay phone stood. Under the dim glow of the streetlight, he fumbled for some change, the metallic clink of coins echoing in the quiet morning. The scent of fresh bread from the bodega mingled with the city's awakening odors, a contrast to the stale, confined air of his apartment.

Dialing O'Brien's number at the precinct, Tony's fingers trembled slightly, his mind racing with thoughts of Cat and the dangers ahead. The phone's cold, metallic surface felt alien against his ear, a stark reminder of the impersonal nature of his plea for help.

His call was answered not by O'Brien, but by the overnight duty officer, a voice unfamiliar yet official. Tony's frustration mounted as he relayed the events of the past night—Cat's abduction and his own harrowing encounter. His voice, tense and hurried, broke slightly as he described the assault, the memory still fresh and painful.

"Please, get this information to Detective O'Brien as soon as possible," Tony implored, his voice carrying a mix of worry and determination. He hung up the phone with a heavy click, a sense of helplessness briefly washing over him as he stepped back onto the dimly lit street.

As Tony stepped away from the bodega's exterior, the morning light washed over him, casting long shadows on the pavement. The city was waking up, its sounds shifting from the quiet of night to the bustling energy of a new day. Cars honked in the distance, and the murmur of early risers filled the air, the smell of coffee and exhaust blending together.

He walked back to his apartment, the urgency of his message to the precinct hanging heavily in his mind. Despite having delivered the information, a sense of helplessness plagued Tony, reliant on the precinct's internal communication to reach O'Brien and uncertain of how quickly they would act.

The surrounding city was coming to life, yet Tony felt isolated in his urgency, keenly aware of every passing minute. With Cat's safety in the balance and the elusive Nomad still at large, the weight of responsibility bore down on him. The sounds of the morning—people chatting, the rattle of delivery trucks, the distant blare of sirens—were a stark reminder that time was moving inexorably forward, with or without him. Like a lone violin playing a solemn tune amidst a grand orchestra's crescendo, Tony's personal urgency contrasted with the city's bustling rhythm, his solitary mission moving against the sweeping tide of the waking metropolis.

Fifty

Schroeder sat alone in her dimly lit apartment, the early morning light struggling to seep through the curtains. The world outside buzzed with the rhythm of another New York day, but inside, a heavy silence prevailed. Schroeder's mind was a torrent of emotions, a mix of grief and relentless determination, following the news of O'Brien's death at the hands of The Nomad.

Her phone rang, piercing the stillness. It was Jensen, the overnight duty officer at the precinct, and a trusted confidant. "Schroeder, it's Jensen. Got a message from Martinez. He's in trouble, says his friend Cat's been kidnapped." Her voice, tinged with a hardened resolve from sleepless nights and a lingering hint of cigarette smoke, was steady.

"I know I'm off the case, Jensen, but I can't ignore this. What did Tony say?"

Jensen relayed Tony's message–the attack he had suffered and Cat's abduction. Each word deepened Schroeder's resolve. Despite being officially off the case, her connection to it, and to the memory of O'Brien, propelled her to act.

After the call, Schroeder stood up, feeling the weight of her suspension like a shadow. Yet, the need to act, to confront the chaos The Nomad had unleashed, was overwhelming. Tony's plight and O'Brien's untimely death had interwoven to form a personal crusade that transcended official duties.

She made her way to Tony's apartment. The city's streets, drenched in the soft light of dawn, felt surreal, almost indifferent to her internal storm. Each step was a silent vow, a promise to O'Brien and the victims, a commitment that went beyond her badge. The cool morning air brushed against her face, carrying the distant sounds of the waking city.

Arriving at Tony's place, she found him visibly battered, the physical testament to his recent encounter. His apartment, chaotic and yet determined, was a mirror to his life–a life now entangled with hers in their hunt for The Nomad.

"Detective Schroeder," Tony began, his voice carrying a mix of surprise and deep-seated concern, "I wasn't expecting you. I've been trying to get ahold of O'Brien."

The weight of the news she carried felt like a physical burden to Schroeder. Drawing a deep breath, she steadied herself. "Tony, there's something you need to know. O'Brien... he's gone. The Nomad got to him."

The words hung in the air, heavy with significance. Tony's face drained of color, his body tensing as he processed the gravity of her words. "Gone? O'Brien's... dead?" His voice was barely above a whisper, laced with a mixture of shock and a creeping sense of reality.

Schroeder's gaze never wavered, though her eyes were a tumultuous sea of emotion. "Yes, and they have suspended me from the force. But I can't just sit on the sidelines. Not with what The Nomad has done, not after O'Brien."

A palpable silence filled the room as they both grappled with the weight of their losses. Tony, still reeling from the shock, looked lost for a moment, his eyes reflecting a deep, personal pain. "Schroeder, I... I don't know what to say. O'Brien was... he didn't deserve this."

Schroeder's voice hardened with resolve, though it trembled slightly with the effort of keeping her emotions in check. "Neither did any of The Nomad's victims. That's why we have to stop him, Tony. For O'Brien, for Cat, for everyone he's hurt."

Tony's expression shifted, a hardened resolve replacing the initial shock. "You're right. We can't let him continue this. We have to stop him, Schroeder."

As they stood amid Tony's apartment, surrounded by the everyday chaos of his life, a solemn understanding passed between them. Schroeder's nod was firm, her resolve clear in her eyes. "Yes, but remember, Tony, we're off the grid now. It's just us, on our own, against him."

Tony met her gaze, his own eyes reflecting a mixture of determination and the weight of the task ahead. "I understand," he said, his voice carrying a newfound gravitas. "We're on our own, but we're not backing down. We'll find The Nomad, no matter what it takes."

Schroeder's expression hardened, mirroring Tony's resolve. "For Cat, for O'Brien," she added, her voice a low, steady promise.

"And for all the lives he's destroyed," Tony continued, his words laden with a deep, personal commitment.

In that small, crowded apartment, amidst the remnants of Tony's daily life, a new alliance forged. An alliance driven by loss and a shared determination to bring an end to The Nomad's reign of terror. Outside, the city carried on, unaware of the resolve being cemented within those four walls. But for Tony and Schroeder, the world had narrowed down to a single, unyielding focus–to bring The Nomad to justice. Like the final, powerful chords of a symphony reaching its climax, their resolve echoed through the stillness of the apartment, signaling the beginning of a relentless pursuit.

Fifty-One

In the muted glow of Tony's apartment, the newly allied duo scrutinized the latest enigmatic note from The Nomad. The paper's crisp texture contrasted with the ominous weight of the words that seemed to taunt them, a sinister puzzle to be solved. Tony, his face etched with a blend of worry and resolve, watched Schroeder closely, the faint scent of coffee lingering in the air.

Schroeder, her detective's eye sharp, read the note aloud, her voice tinged with skepticism and the faint clatter of her pen against the table. " 'The place where light and darkness meet.' It's almost poetic, but what's he really pointing us towards?"

Tony, unable to stay still, paced the room, his footsteps muffled on the worn carpet, his thoughts a whirlwind. "It's cryptic... could be a place of contrasts, somewhere symbolic, perhaps?"

Nodding, Schroeder's gaze remained fixed on the note. "He's playing with us, using our shared past. The Nomad's mind games are part of his signature."

After a few moments, Tony, his brow creased in concentration, broke the silence. "What if it's a literal place? Like, where day and night intersect? Some place that's known for its transitional lighting?" His voice echoed slightly in the sparse room.

Schroeder shook her head, not entirely convinced. "Too vague. The Nomad's smarter than that. He'd want us to think harder." She tapped her pen against the note, a rhythmic sound in the quiet room. "What about a place significant to both of you? A spot from your shared past?"

Tony pondered, then suggested another angle. "Maybe it's metaphorical. Could 'light and darkness' refer to something moral or emotional? A place where good and bad memories collide?"

"That's an interesting angle," Schroeder mused. "Or it might be more abstract. What if 'light and darkness' symbolize knowledge and ignorance? A place related to learning or discovery that you both know?"

Tony leaned back, rubbing his temples, the faint scent of his aftershave mingling with the room's stale air. "Or we could be overthinking it. Maybe it's as simple as a physical space that's half-lit, like an underpass or a tunnel where light barely penetrates."

Schroeder nodded, jotting down each possibility. "All plausible. We need to consider each scenario and see which fits best with what we know about The Nomad."

Their discussion continued, the room filled with the sound of flipping pages and the occasional murmur of contemplation. Each scenario painted a different picture, a potential lead in the labyrinthine game set by The Nomad. With every idea exchanged, they delved deeper into the mind of their adversary, trying to out-think the mastermind who had kept them on their toes.

Then, a memory surged through Tony's mind, halting his steps. "Hold on," he interjected, an idea dawning. "My place I grew up in... it was always gloomy, a mix of shadow and dim light. It could be literal–the convergence of light and dark."

Interest sparked in Schroeder's eyes. "That's a solid lead. Is the building still standing?"

"Yes, but it has been years since I moved out and it was condemned, and nobody has taken care of it. A perfect spot for The Nomad to hide," Tony replied, his voice a mix of hope and trepidation.

"Then we need to go there, see it for ourselves," Schroeder determined, standing up, the sound of her chair scraping against the floor.

Tony paused, the reality of their mission dawning on him. "It's risky. If The Nomad's there..."

"We'll be cautious," Schroeder reassured him, her tone exuding confidence. "But we can't ignore this. It's our best shot at finding Cat and stopping The Nomad."

Together, they gathered essential items–flashlights, first aid supplies, anything that might aid them in an unforeseen encounter. Schroeder checked her personal pistol, which the department didn't pay for, so they didn't take it from her when she was suspended. The gravity of their quest was palpable as they prepared to venture out.

Exiting the apartment, the city's ambient noise wrapped around them, a stark contrast to the quiet determination that had formed between them. They were venturing into a realm both known and unknown, a place shadowed by uncertainty.

The abandoned building, a ghost from Tony's past, now beckoned them–a beacon in their search, a stage for the next act in their pursuit of justice. Like a duo of musicians tuning their instruments before a defining performance, Tony and Schroeder stepped into the streets, their resolve harmonizing with the city's morning symphony, each step a note in their determined melody.

Fifty-Two

As Tony stood before the condemned building, its desolate façade seemed to echo the turmoil within him. The once-familiar structure now loomed like a grim specter from his past, its dilapidated walls merging with the nightmare that had engulfed his present. The surrounding air was heavy with the scent of neglect and decay, a sharp contrast to the crisp autumn breeze outside.

He pushed open the front door, its hinges groaning in protest, the sound reverberating through the empty halls like a sinister prelude. The air inside was stale, thick with the scent of decay and long-forgotten memories. Dust particles danced in the slivers of light that penetrated the gloom, creating a ghostly effect.

Schroeder, her eyes meeting Tony's in a silent vow of unity, circled around to enter from the back. "Keep your eyes open," she murmured, her voice barely audible in the encroaching gloom of twilight. The crunch of gravel under her footsteps faded as she disappeared from sight.

Tony paused for a moment at the threshold of the building, a rush of memories flooding him. The door, hanging askew on its hinges, seemed like a gaping maw to the past. With a deep breath, scented with the musty air of disuse, he crossed the threshold, stepping into the shadowy interior.

The once-vibrant lobby now echoed with emptiness, its worn walls a testament to the passage of time. The dim light filtering through the dirty windows cast eerie patterns on the floor, adding to the sense of foreboding that gripped him.

He began his ascent, the creaking of the old wooden stairs under his feet resonating through the empty building. Each step seemed to echo loudly in the silence, a stark reminder of the desolation surrounding him. The faint, earthy smell of mold lingered in the air, merging with the scent of old wood.

As he climbed, Tony's heart pounded in his chest, his mind racing with possibilities of what awaited him. The faint musty smell of decay filled the air, mingling with the scent of old wood and dust. His skin prickled with unease as he reached the landing of his old floor, the once familiar hallway now a corridor of uncertainty.

Tony advanced cautiously, his every sense alert. The fear of what he might find in his old apartment gnawed at him, a blend of apprehension and an urgent need to find Cat and confront The Nomad. With each step, the memories of his past life in this building collided with the grim reality of his present, creating a dissonance that echoed in the surrounding emptiness.

Tony pushed the door open, the familiar creak now sounding like a warning. The room was mostly shrouded in shadows, the remnants of his past life scattered around in disarray. His heart raced as he scanned the space, the sense of dread mounting with each passing second.

As his eyes adjusted to the dim light, he noticed a faint movement toward his old bedroom. He cautiously made his way towards it, every instinct on high alert. The bedroom door was slightly ajar, and as he pushed it open, a chilling scene unfolded before him.

There, in the room's corner, was Cat, chained to an old radiator, his eyes wide with fear and exhaustion. The sight of his friend in such a state struck Tony with a blend of rage and despair.

"Cat!" Tony exclaimed, rushing to his side. He tried to undo the heavy chains, but his hands shook and he couldn't release them without a key. Instead, he focused on removing the gag from Cat's mouth, his fingers working deftly to loosen the knot.

As the gag came off, Cat coughed and gasped, each breath a struggle. "Tony... he's close... The Nomad," Cat rasped, his voice barely above a whisper.

An icy shiver ran down Tony's spine at the mention of The Nomad. He glanced around the room, half-expecting to see the man materialize from the shadows. "Don't worry, Cat, I'm going to get you out of here," Tony reassured him, though his voice betrayed his own fear.

But before Tony could further assess the situation or comfort Cat, a chilling sensation crept up his spine. He sensed rather than saw someone enter the room. The air seemed to thicken, charged with a malevolent energy.

A cold sensation pressed against Tony's back, the sharp touch of a blade sending a jolt of fear through him. He didn't need to turn around to know who it was. The Nomad's presence was palpable, a chilling shadow that had enveloped them.

The Nomad's voice was a sinister whisper, a sound that made Tony's blood run cold. "You think you can just walk into my domain and win, Tony? This is my game, my rules."

Tony stood rigid, the knife at his back a grim reminder of the precarious situation. He had walked into The Nomad's trap, a carefully laid snare that now threatened to close around them.

Outside, the city's life went on, oblivious to the perilous standoff in the abandoned building. Inside, Tony stood with his back to The Nomad, the architect of his nightmares, in a last confrontation that would decide their fates.

In the waning light of his former home, with Cat's life in the balance and The Nomad's blade at his back, Tony realized that the endgame he had prepared for was more daunting and immediate than he had ever imagined. The irrevocable act of their deadly dance had begun, a crescendo of peril and desperation in a room filled with shadows and fading memories, like the final, haunting notes of a symphony played in a forgotten hall.

Fifty-Three

Detective Schroeder, her trusty Colt Detective Special firmly in hand, advanced with a silent, deliberate resolve towards the rear of the old, decrepit apartment building. The air was heavy with the scent of mold and disrepair, each step a careful movement in a dance with potential danger.

As she pushed open the creaking back entrance, a chorus of hinges singing their age-old song, the world she entered seemed suspended in time. Her flashlight's beam pierced the encompassing darkness, revealing the decay and dust of years gone by. The silence was palpable, broken only by the faint whispers of her own movements through the building.

Moving methodically, her steps precise, mindful of the lurking peril that could hide in any corner, Schroeder navigated the ground floor. Each empty room echoed with the remnants of forgotten stories, the air tinged with the faint, sad scent of lives once lived. Her ear pressed against each sealed door, listening for any hint of movement in the oppressive silence.

Ascending the decaying staircase to the upper levels, her senses heightened, alert for any sign of The Nomad or his captive. The flashlight's beam swept across peeling wallpaper and broken floorboards, the textures of decay painting a grim picture. Despite the pulsing adrenaline, Schroeder's training kept her movements controlled, her breathing steady.

The second floor presented more of the same–locked doors and deserted rooms, each silent space a testament to time's passage. The isolation was almost tangible, yet Schroeder knew she was not alone in this forsaken building.

Upon reaching the third floor, a sense of foreboding gripped her. The sounds of the city below were a distant memory here. Approaching each apartment with heightened caution, she knew that any delay could be critical for Tony and Cat.

A muffled sound halted her–a voice, barely audible yet distinct. Her hand tightened around the revolver's grip; her senses sharpened to a razor's edge. She moved towards the source of the sound, her presence a mere shadow in the gloom.

The door to Tony's old apartment stood ajar, a sliver of light seeping into the dim hallway. Inside, voices could be heard, one unmistakably malicious–The Nomad's. The faint smell of sweat and fear mingled in the air.

Taking a deep breath to steady herself, she prepared for what might lie ahead. In one fluid, decisive movement, she pushed the door open and stepped into the room, her gun at the ready, her eyes quickly scanning the unfolding scenario.

What she saw was a tableau of calculated danger. Tony stood immobilized; a knife pressed against his back by The Nomad. Cat, chained, with a loosened gag around his throat, sat with eyes expressing both fear and a flicker of hope at her arrival.

"Drop the weapon, Detective," The Nomad demanded, his voice unnervingly calm yet tinged with an undercurrent of manic energy. His grip on Tony tightened, a physical manifestation of the turmoil within him.

In that split second, Schroeder evaluated the situation. Her years of experience and finely-honed instincts were all culminating in this crucial moment. "Release him, Nomad," she commanded, her voice firm and authoritative, betraying no hint of fear. "This ends now."

The standoff was a tense, silent symphony, each participant a note in a precarious melody. The Nomad, a discordant chord of chaos; Tony, a note of desperation; Cat, a muted harmony of hope; and Schroeder, the steady rhythm of resolve. In this moment, the crescendo of their confrontation reached its peak, a critical juncture in the night's dark composition.

Fifty-Four

The Nomad's voice, laced with a cold confidence that belied his crumbling sanity, sliced through the tense silence. "Detective, I hold the strings. Their lives," he motioned towards Tony and Cat with his blade, "and yours are mere puppets in my play."

Schroeder's eyes hardened, her mind racing for an edge, a way to destabilize The Nomad. With a calculated risk, she brought up a name she knew would strike a chord. "Tell me, Nomad. What about Emily Caldwell?"

A flicker of shock crossed The Nomad's face, quickly replaced by a sinister grin of recognition at the mention of Emily. "Ah, Emily," he uttered with a disturbing fondness. "Such a delicate, beautiful thing. She was like a flower, resilient yet fragile. But in my hands, she withered."

He leaned in closer, his eyes glinting with madness. "She fought, oh how she fought. It was a dance, really. A dance of wills. But as the days passed, her spirit crumbled. Each tear, each plea, was music to my ears. I watched as hope drained from her eyes, replaced by despair. In the end, she was just a shell, an empty vessel."

The Nomad's twisted recollection of Emily's torment revealed the depth of his derangement. He reveled in the details, lost in his own distorted narrative of the events. "Her last breath," he continued, his voice taking on a dreamy quality, "was a whisper, a sweet surrender to the inevitable. She became part of my tapestry, an exquisite piece of my collection."

Schroeder felt a chilling horror at his words, her heart aching for Emily and the terror she must have endured. Yet, she saw an opening in his ramblings, a chance to use his instability to her advantage. She needed to keep him talking, to find an opening to disarm him.

"And after Emily?" Schroeder prodded; her voice was steady despite the storm of emotions inside her. "What drove you to continue this path of destruction?"

The Nomad's expression shifted, a mix of pride and a strange, melancholic longing. "After Emily, it was as if a dam had broken within me. There was no turning back. Each life I took, each soul I silenced, was a step further into my liberation. Freedom from the mundane, from the chains of ordinary existence."

His words painted a picture of a man lost in his own delusional world, a world where cruelty and control were the guiding forces. Schroeder knew she was walking a tightrope, engaging with a mind unhinged from reality, but it was a risk she had to take to end his reign of terror.

A surge of pain lanced through Schroeder at his admission, confirming her deepest fears about Emily. She swallowed the agony, maintaining her focus. "And the others? The musician, the dancer, Jacky, Tony's mugging, and O'Brien. You masterminded them all?"

The Nomad's grin twisted into something more grotesque, a dark pride seeping into his voice as he recounted his horrific acts. "Each of them, a masterpiece in their own right," he began, his tone disturbingly reverent. "The musician in the park, his melodies silenced forever. The precision of ending his symphony of life, it was... exhilarating."

He shifted slightly, the blade still pressing menacingly against Tony's back. "And the dancer, such grace and poise she had. But in my hands, she was nothing but a puppet. Her movements stilled forever. The way her body collapsed; it was like watching a beautiful performance come to an abrupt, silent end."

The Nomad's eyes gleamed with a sickening joy as he recalled Jacky. "Ah, Jacky. Breaking him like shattering a fragile piece of art. The resilience in his eyes fading to fear, the realization of his helplessness - it was a sight to behold."

His gaze then fell on Tony, a malicious glee in his eyes. "And you, Tony, your beating was just a prelude, a taste of what I could do. The fear in your eyes, the pain, it was just a small part of this grand design."

The Nomad's unsettling recollection took a darker turn as he mentioned Natasha. His eyes, cold and devoid of any humanity, gleamed with a perverse satisfaction. "Your lover," he said, his voice dropping to a sinister whisper. "Her death was a special gift for you, Tony. The way she begged for mercy, the fear in her eyes—it was all for you. I wanted you to feel the pain, the helplessness."

He leaned closer to Tony, his breath foul with the stench of malice. "Seeing her struggle, feeling her life slip away under my grip, it was a moment of profound pleasure. And knowing that her last thoughts were of you, Tony, that made it even more delightful. Her demise wasn't just an end; it was a message, a way to torment you, to show you how powerless you are."

The Nomad's recounting of Natasha's murder was not just a confession; it was a display of his control and manipulation. He savored not only the act of taking a life but also the emotional devastation it wrought on those left behind. His fixation on causing Tony pain revealed a deeper level of his sadistic nature, a chilling insight into the depths of his depravity and the lengths he would go to inflict suffering.

Finally, his thoughts turned to O'Brien, and his smile grew even more sinister. "But O'Brien, oh, he was a special treat. The fight he put up, the defiance in his eyes - it only made his end more satisfying. Watching the life drain from his eyes, feeling him go limp in my grasp, it was a moment of pure, unadulterated bliss."

The Nomad's recounting of his crimes was a window into his twisted soul, each word dripping with a macabre sense of accomplishment. He relished not just the acts themselves, but the emotional and psychological impact they had on his victims and those they left behind. His pleasure in their pain and terror was palpable, a testament to the depth of his depravity.

Revulsion churned in Schroeder's stomach at his callousness, but she masked it with a steely gaze. "You're a monster," she spat out, her voice dripping with contempt. "Your soul is damned."

Unperturbed, The Nomad tightened his grip on Tony. "Maybe so. But not before I complete my grand opus here."

It was clear to Schroeder that reasoning with someone as unhinged as The Nomad was impossible. He was a man lost to his own delusions, unreachable by any plea for humanity. The apartment, once a haven of ordinary life, had become an arena for a harrowing stand-off between life and death.

The atmosphere was thick with the dread of what was to come, a crescendo building in the silent standoff. Schroeder knew she had to act, to disrupt this macabre symphony The Nomad was conducting. In the heart of the darkness, amidst the shadows and memories of the old apartment, the final act of their deadly dance was about to unfold, a crescendo of fate and determination resonating in the charged air.

Fifty-Five

In one fluid, menacing motion, The Nomad altered his stance, bringing the blade's edge perilously close to Cat's exposed neck. The sharp sound of the blade slicing through the air replaced the quietude of the room, as the scales of control balanced precariously. Simultaneously, he thrust Tony with brute force toward Detective Schroeder, the thud of Tony's body resonating in the tense atmosphere.

Regaining his footing, Tony's gaze lifted to meet The Nomad. A torrent of emotions washed over his face–shock, recognition, disbelief–as a buried memory clawed its way to the surface. "I know you," he stammered, his voice trembling, the scent of his fear mingling with the stale air of the room. The man before him, twisted by the passage of time and shadowed by insanity, triggered a forgotten connection from his past.

The Nomad's smile, now a macabre expression of amusement, widened. "Tony, always a step behind. Recall the fire hydrants? The games we played on those streets when we were just kids? Eddie Ortiz ring a bell?" His voice was a haunting melody of the past, tinged with bitterness and loss.

A jolt of realization struck Tony, his heart pounding against his chest, the echo of their childhood laughter resounding in his mind. Eddie Ortiz–the name echoed from the recesses of his childhood, a name once associated with innocent days and shared secrets.

"Eddie?" Tony's voice cracked, his face a tableau of incredulity and shock. "You're Eddie Ortiz? But how? We all thought... we thought you were gone."

Eddie's laughter was a bitter symphony, each note laced with years of pain and resentment. "Died? Far from it, Tony. I had to flee, escape the nightmare. You were there, right alongside me, but you never really saw, did you?"

Tony felt a whirlwind of emotions as he tried to reconcile the innocent boy from his memories with the distorted figure before him. Eddie's revelation unraveled the fabric of his past, leaving him grappling with a reality too painful to comprehend.

Eddie's eyes, cold and devoid of warmth, reflected the venom of his suffering. "I did it, Tony. I killed Arthur Hitchens, took his identity. It was the only way out of the hell I was living in."

"You were my friend, Tony. But you never saw the bruises, never saw the cigarette burns, never heard the cries. You left, and I was left in that hell." His hand quivered, the blade pressing dangerously against Cat's skin. "You were supposed to be my friend."

Schroeder, amidst the unfolding drama, remained focused. Despite the revelations and the tangled past, The Nomad had to be stopped. The risk was too great, the imminent danger too real.

As the past cast its long, dark shadow, the moment of reckoning was upon them. In the dim light of the derelict apartment, friend and enemy, past and present, blurred into a haunting dance. The lines between them, once clear, now intertwined in a complex melody of fate and choice. In this crescendo of confrontation, where childhood memories clashed with present horrors, the imperative was clear—the cycle of violence had to end here, in a final, decisive note of resolution.

Fifty-Six

In the haunting glow of the dimly lit room, Tony stood transfixed, his gaze locked on the distorted form of his childhood companion, Eddie, now the deranged Nomad. The air was thick with the musty scent of decay, a poignant backdrop to the crushing tide of emotions overwhelming Tony - disbelief, shock, and a gnawing guilt that clawed at his conscience.

Eddie's eyes, once windows to a shared bond of friendship, now pierced Tony with an icy, ruthless stare. The knife he brandished gleamed menacingly in the weak light, a tangible symbol of the chasm that yawned open between them. Tony's thoughts swirled in turmoil, a stormy sea of memories and disbelief. The boy he once knew was lost, leaving behind a twisted shadow.

"Dead? Oh, Tony," Eddie said, his voice a sinister whisper that sent chills down Tony's spine. "Death would have been a mercy. Instead, I chose vengeance, a path that led me to you."

Tony's voice was a shattered whisper in the tense air. "Eddie, why? We were like brothers." His heart was a drumbeat of desperation and regret, the sound echoing in the oppressive silence of the room.

Eddie's scornful laughter was a discordant note in the symphony of their past. "Ignorance is no excuse, Tony. My agony was invisible to you. And now, you'll understand true loss."

The room seemed to shrink around them; the walls closing in with the intensity of their confrontation. Tony's breath came in ragged gasps, the air heavy with the weight of a shared history now poisoned by betrayal and pain.

"Decide now, Tony. Save your friend, or save yourself?" Eddie's ultimatum sliced through the air, a sharp note in the crescendo of their final encounter.

At that moment, Tony saw the tragic truth. The Eddie he knew had vanished, consumed by a vortex of pain and anger. In his place stood a specter of vengeance, a man lost to his own darkness. With a heavy heart, Tony replied, "I'm sorry, Eddie. Your path ends here."

The Nomad's face twisted with fury. With a snarl, he released Cat and lunged at Tony, the knife a flash of silver in the dim light. The room became a stage for their climax, a tragic ballet of former friends now locked in a deadly dance. The music of their past, once a harmony of shared experiences, had transformed into a requiem for lost souls, each movement a poignant reminder of what had been and what could never be again.

Fifty-Seven

In that fleeting moment, as chaos unfurled around him, Cat found himself at a crossroads of decision and instinct. His mind raced, adrenaline surging through his veins, even as he lay bound and vulnerable. The chains that had been his confines now glimmered in his mind as potential tools of resistance. It was a sliver of opportunity, but it was all he had.

Cat's mind raced through a kaleidoscope of memories, each vividly recalling the euphoria of his performances, the roar of applause, and the exhilaration of standing on stage. He had always thrived in the spotlight, never backing down from a challenge. But now, the stage he found himself on was far more sinister, the audience replaced by the shadow of death itself.

Memories of his friendship with Tony swirled in his mind, their shared dreams, their mutual support through the highs and lows of their artistic endeavors. They had spent countless nights lost in deep conversation, building a bond that went beyond mere friendship. Tony had always been his anchor, and now, in this dire moment, Cat knew it was his turn to be the rock.

A newfound determination surged within him, pushing back the tide of fear that threatened to engulf him. Cat understood that true courage wasn't about being fearless; it was about facing fear head-on and acting despite it. He couldn't let Tony confront this nightmare alone. He had to act in order to tip the scales in their favor somehow.

Drawing a deep breath, Cat subtly shifted, feeling the unwelcoming chill of the chains binding his wrists. His eyes locked onto the Nomad position, his mind working rapidly to calculate the right moment to strike. This was his chance to reshape the dire narrative unfolding before them.

As the Nomad advanced toward Tony with a predator's grace, Cat launched into action. With every ounce of strength, he possessed, he swung his chained arms, the heavy metal tracing a desperate arc through the air. The chains connected with Eddie, throwing him off balance. The Nomad staggered; his calculated attack disrupted by the unexpected intervention.

In those precious seconds, Cat's brave intervention shifted the dynamics of their perilous situation. It was a striking display of the enduring power of friendship and the resilience of the human spirit. Cat's act of bravery did more than just disrupt The Nomad's assault; it reinforced the unbreakable bond between him and Tony, a bond forged and solidified through shared trials and tribulations.

* * * * *

In the critical moments of the showdown, Schroeder's mind became an island of concentrated resolve amidst the chaos. Time seemed to slow, each second elongating as she meticulously evaluated the rapidly changing scenario. Her extensive experience in law enforcement had honed her for times like these, where any hesitation could spell disaster.

The instant Cat boldly disrupted The Nomad's attack, Schroeder recognized the pivotal opportunity. Instinct and years of tactical training melded into a singular purpose. In scenarios as precarious as this, she knew that swift, decisive action was her most potent weapon.

Schroeder's thoughts were crystal clear, free from any shade of doubt. She had witnessed too much anguish, too much devastation wrought by this man. The Nomad, a phantom from their shared history, had inflicted nothing but pain and turmoil. Deep within, Schroeder understood there was no room for hesitation, no space for leniency. This was the moment to halt his cycle of violence.

Her hand was steady on her Colt Detective Special, its familiar heft anchoring her in the maelstrom. She positioned herself strategically, ensuring her line of sight was unobstructed, her aim unwaveringly fixed on The Nomad. Every ounce of her being was concentrated on this crucial juncture.

As the sound of Cat's chains hitting the floor rang out, Schroeder's finger tensed on the revolver's trigger. The first gunshot broke the heavy air, a sharp report echoing the gravity of the situation. The bullet hurtled forward, a lethal emissary of justice, directed with deadly accuracy.

Without missing a beat, she fired again. Her movements were seamless, the result of ingrained practice. The second shot, as resolute as the first, resonated through the dilapidated structure.

Then came the third shot, a definitive closing note to a prolonged, agonizing ordeal. The room reverberated with the triple discharge; each shot was a testament to Schroeder's unwavering dedication to her duty.

In the ensuing silence, a profound stillness enveloped the room. Schroeder stood resolute, her breathing controlled, her commitment to her role as unwavering as ever. In those decisive moments, her actions had articulated a message of clarity and finality far beyond the capacity of words. The Nomad lay still, his reign of terror conclusively ended.

As the weight of their actions dawned on her, Schroeder experienced a complex mixture of emotions. Relief washed over Schroeder as she realized they had neutralized the immediate threat, but a deep-seated sorrow engulfed her for the lives irreversibly changed and the innocence lost in the violent storm brought upon them by The Nomad.

* * * * *

As Schroeder's revolver discharged, the bullets tore through the air with unyielding force, striking The Nomad— Eddie Ortiz, the boy who had lost himself to darkness. The impact was decisive, and Eddie's body yielded to the brutal finality of the shots, collapsing to the ground in a crumpled heap.

In those last fleeting moments, Eddie experienced a cascade of emotions. Initially, there was shock—a profound disbelief that the end he had orchestrated for others was now his own. He had always seen himself as the orchestrator of this grim saga, but now, as he lay on the cold, hard floor, the knife slipping from his weakening grasp, the stark reality of his mortality was undeniable.

Eddie's eyes, wide with a newfound understanding of his fate, frantically scanned the room. His gaze flitted over Tony, Cat, and Schroeder, seeking something—perhaps a glimmer of understanding or forgiveness, or maybe just an ultimate recognition of his tormented existence.

The physical pain from the gunshot wounds was intense, but it was the emotional agony that truly engulfed him. His mind raced through a life marred by abuse, neglect, and a desperate quest for escape. He reflected on his childhood with Tony, their once innocent bond, and how it contrasted with the distorted path he had chosen.

As Eddie lay dying, a deep sense of regret enveloped him. He realized the futility of his vengeful crusade, the senseless cycle of violence he had perpetuated. There was a fleeting yearning for redemption, a wish that he had chosen a different path, one that might have led to a different end.

But such realizations came too late. The world around him dimmed, the sounds of the room fading into a distant, hollow echo. Eddie's hold on life was slipping away, the peripheries of his vision darkening into nothingness.

With his final breath, a whisper escaped his lips— perhaps an apology, perhaps a name, lost to the void that swiftly enveloped him. And then, with one last shudder,

Eddie's life ebbed away, bringing The Nomad's twisted journey to its inevitable, tragic end.

The knife clattered to the ground beside him, a tangible remnant of a soul lost to despair, as Eddie lay motionless. His eyes, which had once burned with pain and fury, now stared emptily, devoid of life, into a world beyond his reach.

Outside, the relentless rhythm of the city marched on, oblivious to the drama that had just concluded within the decrepit building. Inside, Eddie, the boy who had morphed into The Nomad, lay defeated, his story concluding not with a resounding climax, but with a subdued, somber whisper.

* * * * *

The aftermath of the gunfire left Tony's heart thundering in his chest, a wild drumbeat echoing his shock and adrenaline surge. In the split second when The Nomad had charged, instinct had kicked in, priming him for a grim finale that was abruptly averted by Schroeder's decisive shots.

As Eddie's body crumpled to the ground, a surreal sense of disbelief engulfed Tony. His mind reeled, struggling to grasp the whirlwind of events–the childhood companion he had rediscovered as The Nomad was now a lifeless figure on the floor. The room spun, the reverberating gunshots intertwining with the stark reality of Eddie's demise.

Automatically, Tony moved towards Cat, still bound and visibly shaken. With hands that trembled yet moved with determined urgency, he worked to free his friend from the chains that had ensnared him. The clinking of the metal chains as they hit the floor shattered the heavy silence, a resounding symbol of their newfound liberation.

As the chains fell away, Cat collapsed, his body wracked by the ordeal. Tony caught him, supporting him in a firm, reassuring embrace. Cat's body quivered, overwhelmed by a torrent of fear and relief, and Tony felt the weight of his friend's vulnerability.

Tony's emotions were a tumultuous mix of relief and grief. Relief that Cat was safe, that Schroeder had intervened just in time, that their nightmare was finally over. Yet, there was also a deep sense of mourning for the innocence of his past, now forever marred by the truth of Eddie's twisted journey.

Holding Cat, Tony's gaze turned to Eddie's still form. Memories cascaded through his mind–their carefree childhood days, shared adventures, a bond that once seemed unbreakable, now juxtaposed against the grim reality of Eddie's end. The room, once a haven of youthful joy, now felt like a somber mausoleum, echoing the tragic conclusion of a friendship destroyed by darkness.

Outside, life in the city marched on, oblivious to the drama that had unfolded within these walls. Inside, however, time seemed to pause, the remnants of their confrontation a stark reminder of the destructive path The Nomad had forged.

In this poignant moment, Tony confronted the full weight of his journey–a path that had led him back to his roots, only to uncover a past irrevocably tainted. The resolution of The Nomad's terror brought no solace, merely a sobering realization of a chapter concluded in the most definitive, tragic manner.

Fifty-Eight

In the wake of The Nomad's downfall, a shadow lingered over those who had endured his terror. Though physically unharmed, Jacky and Cat found themselves ensnared in the aftermath of their harrowing experiences, each grappling with the unseen scars left behind.

* * * * *

Jacky, once the embodiment of free spirit and energy, navigated uncharted waters. The assault by The Nomad left no physical marks, yet it scarred his psyche in deep, profound ways.

He wrestled with an unfamiliar vulnerability, a jarring contrast to his usual fearless attitude. The nights, his former playgrounds of musical expression, now harbored shadows and lurking threats. His Stratocaster, which once joyously resonated with his touch, now sometimes recalled the chilling grip of The Nomad's wire.

Despite these internal storms, Jacky turned to his music, seeking solace, albeit now tinged with the remnants of his trauma. The stage, once a realm of liberation, occasionally transformed into an arena of his exposed vulnerabilities. Yet, he continued, his music infused with a newfound emotional depth, resonating with his journey of healing.

Friends and fans noted a change–a reflective, introspective layer new to Jacky. Therapy sessions, initially met with reluctance, gradually became a space for healing, allowing Jacky to vocalize and confront his fears and anxieties.

* * * * *

Cat, too, carried indelible marks from his near-death experience. He physically bounced back; emotionally, the ordeal's shadows lingered. He experienced spikes of intense anxiety, a foreign sensation that ambushed him without warning.

Cat's resilience, a defining trait, became his lifeline. His bond with Tony, strengthened in the furnace of shared trauma, became a pillar of support. Their evenings were filled with conversations, a mutual exchange of experiences and understanding that fostered healing.

Music became Cat's therapeutic outlet, his guitar playing reflecting his emotional journey. His performances, always heartfelt, now echoed with the depth of his experiences.

Reflective and thoughtful, Cat's journey became an inspiration to others facing their own battles. His resilience shone like a beacon of hope, illustrating the power of the human spirit in overcoming adversity.

* * * * *

For both Jacky and Cat, The Nomad's legacy was a complex interweaving of fear, resilience, and the indomitable human spirit. Their experiences, though marred by terror, became integral to their narratives, shaping them in unforeseen ways.

They marched forward, carrying the scars of their past, but also a newfound gratitude for life's present moments. Their survival was a testament to their inner strength, and through their music, conversations, and triumphs, they echoed a resonant message: In even the darkest times, there is a path to healing, a chance for redemption, and a melody of hope that plays on.

Fifty-Nine

In the reflective quiet of her apartment, Schroeder found herself caught in a rare current of introspection. The saga of The Nomad's case unfolded in her mind, a complex narrative woven with personal loss and professional struggle. This case had transcended the pursuit of justice; it had become an introspective journey, compelling her to face the phantoms of her past and reassess her future trajectory.

Sitting by the window, the sprawling cityscape before her, Schroeder pondered the case's closure. It was a journey that had left deep imprints on her, both in her career and her inner world. Emily Caldwell's fate, entwined tragically with The Nomad's terror, had reopened long-sealed chambers of her heart.

The resolution of Emily's story tinged the closure with sorrow and a profound sense of what had been irretrievably lost. Learning of Emily's fate as a victim of The Nomad had reopened old wounds, but it also granted Schroeder a bitter sense of closure, enabling her to finally turn a page that had remained unturned for far too long.

In the case's aftermath, Schroeder rejoined the police force after her suspension. Her return was met with respect and acknowledgment of her unwavering commitment and skill. Yet, as days melted into weeks, a seed of restlessness germinated within her, a longing for something new, a change.

The Nomad case had kindled in Schroeder an intense interest in the psychological underpinnings of criminal behavior. She found herself immersed in literature on forensic psychology and criminal profiling, fascinated by the complex tapestry of the criminal psyche.

This newfound interest prompted a significant career decision. With a blend of enthusiasm and apprehension, Schroeder applied to the FBI, drawn to the challenge of their forensic profiling team. The application process was demanding, but she met each challenge with her characteristic determination and grit.

Upon her acceptance, Schroeder faced the bittersweet decision of leaving the police force. It was a departure marked not by regret but by a readiness for growth and exploration. Joining the FBI represented a new frontier, an opportunity to delve into the depths of criminal psychology.

As she readied herself for the upcoming training and trials at the FBI, Schroeder felt a rejuvenating sense of purpose, a readiness to embrace this new chapter. Her experiences as a detective had fortified her, equipping her with the resilience and insight needed for the challenges ahead.

Gazing out at the city, a metropolis she had served with dedication and bravery, Schroeder felt a profound sense of gratitude. The city, like a vast orchestra, had played a symphony of experiences in her life–some notes were harsh and dissonant, others harmonious and uplifting. Now, as she prepared to leave the NYPD, it felt like the closing of a grand, intricate composition, one that had shaped her very essence. Ahead of her lay a new melody, a fresh score to be written with the FBI. This new chapter promised unexplored territories in the vast realm of law enforcement and criminal psychology, offering a chance to add new rhythms and harmonies to her life's ongoing symphony.

Sixty

In the shadow of the events that had irrevocably changed his world, Tony wandered through his days, lost in a whirlpool of emotions. The sting of Natasha's loss, the shattering revelation of Eddie's descent into The Nomad, and the aftermath of their last confrontation weighed heavily on his soul.

Every day felt like a surreal journey through a landscape that had lost its color and vibrancy. Memories of Natasha, vibrant and full of life, now flickered like ghostly images in a world he could no longer touch. Her laughter, once a melody that filled his life, had faded into a haunting refrain of what could have been. The truth about Eddie, once his childhood confidant, now The Nomad, left a deep chasm in his heart, tearing apart the tapestry of his boyhood memories.

As if these emotional trials weren't enough, the harsh reality of life intruded unceremoniously. Tony found himself evicted from his apartment, a cruel reminder of how drastically his life had spiraled out of control. The streets of New York, which once echoed with his dreams and ambitions, now seemed to turn a blind eye to his despair.

Yet, in the depths of this darkness, Tony found a glimmer of light in the music trapped in his soul. He turned to his new, borrowed bass guitar, his fingers strumming and picking at the strings, weaving his pain, his loss, and his longing for healing into a poignant symphony of his experiences. His music became his refuge, a means to navigate the storm of his emotions.

The songs he wrote and played were cathartic, each note a step towards mending the fractures in his spirit. They spoke of his struggles, his journey through the valley of shadows, and his quest for a semblance of peace. The melodies were bittersweet, a fusion of sorrow and hope, echoing his tumultuous journey towards finding a fresh path in life.

Through music, Tony stitched together the fragments of his shattered world. It was a slow, arduous process, filled with moments of despair and flashes of hope. But in each chord and lyric, Tony found a piece of himself, a resilient spirit that refused to be silenced by the chaos that had engulfed his life.

Sixty-One

In the chaos' wake that had upturned his life, Tony grasped at the lifeline extended by Mikhail. Moving into his friend's modest apartment offered a semblance of normalcy and stability amidst the tumult. The space, though small, radiated a warmth and comfort that Tony sorely needed, a safe harbor from the storm that raged within him.

As they cohabited, their evenings often stretched into nights filled with deep conversations and reflections. They dissected the surreal events that had unfolded, pondering over the twists of fate and the raw hand they'd been dealt. Mikhail, steadfast and understanding, became the anchor Tony clung to in these turbulent times.

Mikhail, too, was at a crossroads, feeling the pull of a new beginning away from the city that had been their stage for both triumph and tragedy. He spoke of moving to the West Coast, a land of sun and endless possibilities, seeking to carve out a new path and perhaps find a peace that New York could no longer offer.

For Tony, Mikhail's companionship during this period was more than just a comfort; it was a lifeline. In the quiet solidarity of their shared space, they spoke of dreams yet unfulfilled, of melodies yet unsung, and of roads yet untraveled. Mikhail's presence was a balm to Tony's frayed spirit, a reminder that the end of one chapter heralds the start of another.

The day Mikhail departed for the West Coast was laden with a mix of emotions. It was a farewell to the shared experiences that had defined a significant part of their lives. Yet, there was an undercurrent of hope–a sense that this separation was not an end, but a segue into new beginnings for both of them. Their goodbye was not just a parting but a pledge to maintain the bond that adversity had strengthened, a connection that would endure the miles and the changes that lay ahead.

As Tony watched Mikhail leave, he felt a surge of mixed emotions - loss, hope, and a renewed sense of purpose. Their journey together had been a testament to the power of friendship in the face of life's storms. And as he stood in the doorway of what was now his temporary home, Tony realized that this was just another turn in the road, a bend that led to new horizons and possibilities, both for himself and for Mikhail. The future was uncertain, but it held the promise of new music, new dreams, and a continuation of the journey they had started together.

Sixty-Two

In the dwindling days of her time in New York, Tony sought a meeting with Schroeder at a quaint coffee shop, nestled amidst the bustling streets of the city. This rendezvous was more than a casual encounter; it was a necessary epilogue to the saga that had intertwined their lives.

As they sat across from each other, the clatter of the café fading into a soft backdrop, Schroeder, on the cusp of a new chapter with the FBI, lent an empathetic ear to Tony. She listened as he poured out his heart, sharing the tumult of his emotions and his aspirations that flickered like dim stars in the aftermath of a storm.

Perceiving the latent potential in Tony, and understanding his deep-seated need for purpose and direction, Schroeder offered a suggestion that would pivot the trajectory of his life. "Tony, have you ever thought about becoming a private investigator?" she asked, her voice imbued with genuine confidence in his capabilities.

The proposition resonated with Tony, striking a harmonious chord within him. The skills he had sharpened during his harrowing search for The Nomad, his intimate acquaintance with loss and the thirst for justice, all seemed to converge towards this new avenue.

Buoyed by Schroeder's unwavering belief in him, Tony embarked on the journey to get his private investigator's license. The path was arduous, dotted with obstacles and challenges, but it provided a much-needed focus, a melody to follow amidst the cacophony of his recent life.

As he stood on the threshold of this new endeavor, Tony felt a cautious optimism lighting his way. The road ahead was uncharted, replete with potential challenges and unknowns, yet it beckoned with the promise of new narratives, the opportunity to channel his experiences in aiding others.

Their last conversation at the coffee shop marked a significant crescendo in Tony's life, a moment that solidified his determination to forge a new path. In the embrace of New York City, with its relentless pulse and vibrant life all around them, Tony discovered a renewed sense of tranquility and a clear direction.

With his bass guitar as his constant companion and a fresh purpose igniting his soul, Tony stepped into the future, leaving the shadowy corridors of his past behind. The adversities he had weathered and the wisdom he had garnered sculpted Tony's journey, now his to define. The specter of The Nomad, while a part of his history, would not cast its pall over his future. Poised to face the world anew, Tony embraced his next chapter, his spirit echoing the resilient chords of hope and renewal.

Acknowledgement

To my father, who helped determine how police officers operated in the 1970s, thank you.

To Nathan, who helped me finish this novel on its umpteenth rewrite, thank you.

To Lisa, snarf.

To Jerri, who put up with me ignoring her so I could put all my time and energy into writing, thank you.

To my youngest, Quinn, who I asked to not play their musical instruments at night or on the weekends, while I was creating, thank you. I understand that this was as hard for you as it was for me, since like my writing, your music has to come out.

About the Author

N.R. Willick has been accused of a lot of things in his life- refusing to release the secrets on how the Pyramids were built; being the lyrical force behind Led Zeppelin; and knowing where all the bodies are buried.

However, all he will admit to is: He has been a closet writer for over three decades; being tall; having three children and two purr babies; not planning on running for the American presidency; finally completing his first novel, *Bass Rift*; and confirming he is the reason no one worries about quicksand or The Bermuda Triangle any longer. He lives in Northern California, and can be reached at his website, nrwillick.com